NEVER TOO LATE FOR LOVE

Tiffany and Jason sat in the pew as they listened to the couple exchange wedding vows.

"My love," the woman said, her rich voice filling the church. "I am blessed that you are the one whom I choose to trust, to love, and to endure whatever comes. You've taught me that it's never too late for happiness, never too late for my heart to be filled with joy, never too late for love. I make a covenant to honor, respect and above all to love you for the rest of my journey through this life and forevermore."

Tears filled Tiffany's eyes. Never too late.

"In mutual fidelity I present these rings," the minister said.

"I give you this ring as I give you my heart, and with it I wed you and pledge you my love forever." He placed the ring on her finger.

"I give you this ring as I give you my heart, and with it I wed you and pledge you my love forever."

"And now since you have pledged yourselves to each other in the presence of this company," the minister said, "I do by virtue of the authority vested in me, pronounce you husband and wife."

As they kissed, Tiffany started to reach for Jason's hand, but instead clasped her hands together, the yearning in her own heart near exploding. What would she give to experience a moment as deep and sacred and love-filled as the couple before her experienced? She'd made so many mistakes, followed so many wrong paths. The man she'd given her youth to had no heart to give her. And so she lost her own heart. The years and alcohol had turned her despair and loneliness into numbness. But now she was alive again and the man at her side ... She dared not hope. Was it ever too late to find your heart again?

NEVER TOO LATE FOR LOVE

Monica Jackson

ARABESQUE
BOOKS

BET Publications, LLC
www.msbet.com
www.arabesquebooks.com

ARABESQUE BOOKS are published by

BET Publications, LLC
c/o BET BOOKS
One BET Plaza
1900 W Place NE
Washington, D.C. 20018-1211

BET Books is a trademark of Black Entertainment Television, Inc. ARABESQUE, the ARABESQUE logo and the BET BOOKS logo are trademarks and registered trademarks.

First Printing: June, 2000
10 9 8 7 6 5 4 3 2 1

Printed in the United States of America

To Amethyst Rose, my love, my light, and the center of my life

Chapter 1

Twelve hours of gritty highway miles filled with adrenaline-charged anticipation had rolled by for Tiffany Eastman. She didn't put the pedal to the metal on the trip north from Atlanta like she usually did. She drove just below the posted speed limit. It wasn't that she didn't want to hurry to her new life in St. Louis. No, it was that she didn't want to mess it up. A speeding ticket would be a bad omen, an accident disastrous.

She hit the outskirts of the city and it had been standard mid-American suburbs. But now she was entering the St. Louis city limits and there was a feel that Atlanta, with its brassy, modern confidence, lacked. Tiffany rolled down the windows to let out the recycled air-conditioned atmosphere and to smell the city. Each city had its own unique smell, and St. Louis's odor hit her immediately. Hops. This whole end of the city smelled like beer. Not the woozy, fetid odor that came off human breath, but a rich wheaty smell. Anheuser-Busch had put its stamp on the very air.

St. Louis was weathered brick and ornate Gothic cathedral lattice, old and lived-in, with the feel of history, character and distinct cultural influences. Overlaying the city was something like the tarnish of middle age, as if it had moved a bit beyond its prime and the kids had moved on to bigger and better things. There was a sense of stagnation, a palpable aura of waiting. The city seemed to beg for something to grant it a new chance to regain its former vigor and energy.

After forty-seven years of living, Tiffany identified with the city. She pressed on the gas pedal incrementally. Suddenly she couldn't wait. In a few minutes she'd be face to face with the man she'd met just weeks before in Atlanta. Was there such a thing as love at first sight? When she first saw Jason he'd rung the doorbell of her Atlanta apartment early one morning. His daughter Taylor, her roommate and surrogate daughter, had still been in bed. Tiffany had pulled open the door and their eyes met and held for a second. She dropped her eyes, feeling confused. When she raised her eyes again and met his, she perceived warm brown pools of knowing, of caring, of kindness, affection, maturity and the possibility of love. At that very moment she knew he was the one.

Tiffany turned onto Lindell Avenue. The big things to be nervous about, a new job, another city, all the new beginnings were a static hum in the background of her present anxiety. She was going to see Jason Cates again. She bit her lip and shook her head, bringing herself back to the present and putting wishes, hopes and longings out of her mind.

She caught her breath as Jason's imposing brick house came into view. Set back from a wide boulevard with other large homes, each one unique, old oak trees lined the front drive and the brick walls were covered with ivy. A large screen enclosed the front porch where she could see a porch swing and a wicker table and chairs. It had an old-fashioned Victorian aura, although with none of the effete, over-studied elegance Victoriana sometimes held.

This house was meant for a family, preferably a loud, raucous one with young kids with muddy feet and large slobbery dogs. She couldn't imagine a single widower living here alone. She pulled up in front of the house, cut the motor and took a deep breath. She got out of the car. This was it. When she rang the doorbell, the chime reverberated through the house as it echoed through her own body. She listened intently for the sound of footsteps, but they failed to come. She rang the doorbell again. And waited. The sun was setting and the day deepened into blue. Jason wasn't home.

She fumbled for the key in her purse. He'd sent a key for that contingency. She had hoped she wouldn't have to use it. Using a key to get into his house felt too intimate. It felt as if she really knew him, as if she belonged, as if . . . she were coming home.

She pushed the door shut behind her. A sudden fear rushed through her that maybe Jason was in the house and would surprise her as if she were a burglar. "Jason?"

No answer. Her Nikes were soundless on the highly polished wood floor of the foyer. A dining room with an ornate crystal chandelier was to the left. The fancy lighting fixture was out of place with a well-used, scarred table surrounded by sturdy wood chairs that had seats covered with worn and faded striped fabric.

Off to the right, a large, well-used fireplace with a beautiful ornate wood mantel graced the room. That was the only thing fancy about it. It was a room also furnished for comfort rather than décor, from the earth-toned plush carpet to the brown overstuffed couch and chairs and a large recliner that lorded over the other furniture.

The kitchen's appliances were harvest gold that said "seventies" along with the white gold and avocado kitchen table. The cabinets were dark oak and had likely been in place since the house was built. Jason said a housekeeper came daily, and the kitchen was spotlessly clean.

There were two bedrooms downstairs, both exactly the same size and both with bathrooms off of them. One was done in matching blue. Blue walls, blue bedspread, blue carpet, a surfeit of blueness. Tiffany remembered Jason saying blue was his favorite color. Must be true.

The other bedroom was as bland as a motel room. Tan carpet, tan chenille bedspread, off-white walls with no pictures, wooden dresser, chest of drawers and headboard that could have been ordered off the floor of any Sears in the country. This must be the guest bedroom.

Several hours later, Tiffany sat in the big recliner and watched the late night news go off. She hadn't heard from him. The phone had rung twice and she'd been nervous about answering it. The answering machine kicked in. One of Jason's sons had called. Taylor had called wondering if she had gotten there safely, and she called her back. Taylor reassured her that it was likely her father had been delayed by surgery.

Exhaustion had set in. She reached for the remote, flicked the television off, yawned and stretched. She was going to take a shower and turn in. She felt both disappointed and relieved that she hadn't seen Jason yet. Tomorrow she'd be much fresher. A small smile played over her features. She couldn't wait.

Jason Cates pulled up to his home feeling weary. His scheduled surgeries had taken longer than planned, and then an emergency surgery had lasted long into the night. A man too young to be felled by a heart attack. He did the best he could and turned the man's fate over to God. That should have been enough, and a long time ago it would have been, but now . . . his faith had wavered and doubts and worries lingered.

He narrowed his eyes at the dark red Toyota Camry in his driveway. Tiffany Eastman must have arrived already. He'd been hoping he would get home in time to welcome her. He pulled into his garage and closed his eyes for a moment, relaxing in the custom leather seats. What had he been thinking when he asked Tiffany to stay with him until she found a place? What was he thinking when he lobbied so hard to get her that job offer with WomenHelp, Inc. in St. Louis in the first place?

Jared, his son, had raised an eyebrow when he'd heard that his sister's much older roommate was moving from Atlanta. "Dad, you must really want that woman with all the changes you're going through to get her up here."

Jason had frowned at him and Jared never mentioned the topic again. Of course he didn't "want" Tiffany Eastman. He'd do the same thing for anyone. Wouldn't he?

He went into the dark house. The fluorescent numbers of his watch glowed 11:55 P.M. Tiffany had probably settled down after her long drive. He'd told the cleaning lady to freshen the guest room and pull the bedding back for her.

Just as well, he was beat. Relieved that the social niceties could wait until tomorrow, he walked into his bedroom, pulling his tie off. He stripped down to his briefs and dropped his clothes neatly on the chair without turning on the lights. His suit was due to go to the cleaners anyway.

He reached for the bedding and felt that the covers were already pulled back. His new cleaning lady had it on the ball, he thought, and he made a note to give her a raise as a token of his appreciation of the little extras she did.

He slid into his bed and let out a groan of pleasure at the feel of the cool, clean sheets. A yelp next to his ear shattered the dark quiet of the room. What the—? He jumped straight up and yelled back. What was it? An animal? An intruder?

"What are you doing in my bed?" a hoarse feminine voice demanded.

Tiffany. Relief was followed by irritation, and he reached to turn on the bedside lamp. Light flooded the room and he stared into her big brown eyes.

Her chest was . . . what was the right word? Heaving. He quickly averted his eyes from her breasts.

"I think I should be asking that question."

"This is your bed?"

"Yes, this is my bed."

She blinked at him with not a trace of apology or modesty in her eyes. He'd thought the woman had class.

"I had no idea it was your bed. I thought this was the guest room," she said.

"The guest room is down the hall to your left."

"Oh. The very blue room."

"One of my sons redecorated it." He drew away from her.

"Sorry, I made a mistake. It isn't like I snuck into your bed to assault you or anything."

His eyes widened. "I-I couldn't imagine such a thing. Well, I could, but . . . but . . . ."

"You seem upset. I apologize for upsetting you."

Her calm voice flustered him even more. "I'm not upset, I'm surprised at finding a strange woman in my bed."

"I said I didn't know it was your bed."

"Yeah, that was what you said."

She slid out of the bed and stood beside it, shivering slightly in the air-conditioning. She wore a big wrinkled white T-shirt. Her hair was standing on end and he'd never seen her without makeup before. Her flawless Hershey-brown skin didn't need it. He'd forgotten how beautiful she was. He also noticed the outline of brightly colored panties, fuchsia maybe, and hard erect nipples through the soft white cotton. God help him. He stood on the other side of the bed and grabbed a pillow to cover his midsection.

"Do you need me to show you the way to the guest bedroom?" he asked.

"I think I can manage it."

"Well?"

She turned and flounced away, attitude quivering in every outraged movement of her body. Her high, round butt twitched with each step.

He fell back in the bed after he heard the guest bedroom door slam.

Jason swallowed. He'd handled it poorly. He'd looked forward all day to seeing her again. But finding her in his bed had disconcerted him badly. No woman had graced his bed for years. That's not saying he hadn't had his share of liaisons, but they had always been on someone else's turf, in someone else's bed. That had been one of his rules.

What made it worse was that she looked so good. This was going to be a challenge, all right. The first woman in his house other than his daughter in thirty years was a firecracker and fine to boot. He thought of her gorgeous eyes and her womanly, trim shape outlined by the thin cotton T-shirt, and he groaned. A challenge indeed.

Tiffany punched her pillow and thrashed around to lay on her other side. Jason Cates had looked at her as if she sneaked into his bed to rape his old rear end. She rolled back over on her back and stared into the gray darkness of the ceiling above. He had the nerve to ask her, "What are you doing in my bed?"

What do you think, old man? I thought a quick knock of the boots would get us off on the right . . . er, foot, if you know what I mean. Yep, that's what she should have said. Bet she'd be calling 9-1-1 right now because of the heart attack he would have had.

Tiffany grinned into the darkness. No, she didn't want him to die yet. The man was too fine. Jason Cates was a widower, a fifty-five-year-old successful cardiovascular surgeon who had managed to stay single for the past thirty years. He took her breath away with skin as smooth as milky chocolate and a full head of hair, touched with gray with distinguished white flags at his temples. He was tall and long-legged and had a muscled chest, strong arms and washboard abs. He had the build of a thirty-five-year-old.

When Jason called a couple of weeks after she'd met him in Atlanta and told her about a job opening in St. Louis, she knew destiny was holding out a brass ring for her and it was up to her to reach out and grab it.

It seemed as if fate were writing the script. Everything fell into place without even a nudge needed. She'd attended Spelman College more than twenty-five years ago with the woman who interviewed her for the job in St. Louis. The job offer came quickly and she'd accepted immediately. When Jason mentioned casually, "Why don't you stay with me until you find a place of your own," she thought she'd have a stroke then and there. Getting her set up with a job and a place to stay seemed like more than kindness.

Another change, another chance. She'd heard even good changes were stressful, and in the past three years she'd had more than her share of upheavals. She'd left a marriage, lost a husband, lost a home, changed cities, changed jobs, changed lifestyles. It had all been for the best, but . . . like St. Louis, she was a little past her prime, but by no means out of gas. She still sought renovation of the soul and cherished the dream of happiness within a relationship. She'd never stopped believing in love.

At first sight, she trusted Jason, mind, heart, body and soul. There was no reason or logic to it; it was a simple fact. But she wouldn't argue if someone told her she was stupid to trust a man. No man she'd given her trust to before to any degree had lived up to it. But giving into hopelessness would mean she allowed bitterness and regrets to swallow her up.

Somewhere inside her were the hopes of a girl. A girl who still longed to be loved and knew with every cell in her body that love was possible and that love was going to happen to her. She prayed things worked out. She had already experienced enough pain to last a lifetime. She shut her eyes.

It felt like only a few moments later, but the cold morning dawn light shone through the window as Tiffany opened her eyes. She must have slept in spite of her upset. She got up and used the bathroom, then returned and climbed back under the covers. She usually was an early riser, but this morning, it wouldn't hurt to see if she could catch a few extra winks. In the back of her mind she knew she was anxious about seeing Jason again in the light of day. It didn't hurt to put it off for as long as she could, did it?

Chapter 2

Jason looked at his watch. It was almost noon. Why in God's name was the woman still in bed? He'd thought when he met her in Atlanta that she was an early riser like him. An industrious, organized person. He'd thought very highly of her. Perhaps he'd been wrong. Perhaps he'd been wrong about a lot of things about her.

She'd unsettled him more than any other woman had that he could remember. He had order in his life, a place for everything. Most of all, he had his priorities. His children came foremost, first and always. He'd raised six children, most of them still in diapers, without a mother. His job, which was more of a calling, a ministry, was next. At the very bottom of his list came diversions like women. Not that the occasional diversion didn't have its place. That was the key, its place.

The place for diversions of the womanly sort had never been the home he built with his wife more than thirty years ago, or the bedroom they had shared. He'd imagined for years that the spirit of his wife lingered in the house, urging him on, supporting him, encouraging him. Now, ever since all the kids had grown up and left, all that seemed to remain of her was the dusty echo of his memories.

But it still was her house. Deep within, he still felt he'd violated something when he'd allowed another woman within her walls. Let another woman in the room where they'd shared a bed. He sighed as he heard a shower come on. Finally Tiffany was awake. He hurried to the kitchen to put on a pot of coffee. What he'd done was done. Now, it was up to him to make the best of things.

Tiffany rolled over and squinted against the sun pouring through the open blinds. She'd better get up. She really didn't want to. The fevered pitch of hopeful anticipation she'd felt yesterday had dulled to a nagging anxiety.

She'd been worried about making a good initial impression on Jason and she was afraid she'd made an awful one. She could have kicked herself for not bothering to hang up some of her things. She would have seen Jason's clothes hanging in the closet and she would have known it was his room.

She sat up in her bed. It was time to get dressed and face the day. She'd have to brave Jason's room again. Her bags were in there. When she carried them in, she simply dumped them by the closet. Tugging at her T-shirt, she peeked out of her room and spied her bags set neatly outside her door. With a sigh of relief she dragged them into the room.

She showered, then tried several outfits before choosing the casual khaki Bermuda shorts, a polo shirt and sandals. Checking herself out in the mirrored closet doors, Tiffany told herself that she looked good.

She took a deep breath and headed out of the room. The smell of coffee drew her toward the kitchen. Jason was standing at the stove. He sensed her presence and turned and nodded at her with a pleasant smile. Then he dropped a bowl of chopped vegetables into the hot oil and the sizzling aroma that rose made her stomach grumble.

"Since it's almost noon, I thought I'd make omelets for lunch. Vegetables, cheese, Canadian bacon. Does that sound all right to you?"

"Sounds great."

"The cups are in the cabinet to the right of the sink."

She got out a mug and poured a cup of coffee. The half-and-half was on the top shelf of the fridge. She liked that. She always preferred half-and-half over plain milk in her coffee. Never mind the calories.

She settled down and watched Jason expertly handle the food. The man could cook; she had to give him that. She wondered if she should mention the mishap of last night, slip in an apology or let it go like it never happened.

"I'm sorry I was so grouchy last night," Jason said. "It had been a long day and a frustrating one. It was touch-and-go with a patient."

Tiffany studied his profile as he flipped the omelet. Unshaved and casually dressed in jeans, T-shirt and bare feet, he looked . . . sexy, downright sexy. His feet matched his surgeon's fingers, long, elegant and cared for but not manicured or foppish. A workingman's hands and feet with breadth in addition to length.

"Do you want to talk about it?"

He shrugged and put two English muffins in the toaster. "I'm past the point where talking makes a whole lot of difference. People die. All I can do is to turn it over to God and know I did the best I could."

"You never have a sense of failure?"

He looked at her and turned away to slide the omelet on a plate. The muffins popped up and he put two plates on the table along with knives and forks. "Of course I feel like I failed sometimes. It's just never helped me to talk about it."

Tiffany felt like she was floundering badly with him. She intuited there was something going on with him under the words, but she didn't have the foggiest idea what.

He reached in the refrigerator for a bowl of cut fresh fruit and butter and sat across from her. He bowed his head to pray before his meal. Tiffany felt awkward for a moment, then joined him. She served herself a generous portion of the delicious-looking omelet and slathered the hot muffin with butter. "This meal looks wonderful. Thank you."

"Quick and easy. I wrote the book on how to cook a meal in fifteen minutes or less."

"Did you do the cooking for the family or did you have a cook?"

"I had a housekeeper who would pinch-hit for me if I needed it, but I usually cooked myself. I enjoy it. Now, cleaning—I'll gladly let someone else take care of that."

"The omelet is delicious."

They ate in silence. Tiffany occasionally felt Jason's eyes on her. She tried not to squirm. His glance wasn't admiring like it was when she first met him in Atlanta. It was rather assessing. Should she move to a hotel instead of staying with him until she found a place? She hoped she wouldn't have to. But she wanted to stay here in this wonderful, rambling, ivy-covered house. It wasn't a place you could imagine ghosts haunted despite the Victorian touches and slightly Gothic look the intricate brickwork and turrets gave it. It was a friendly house, and the only ghosts were the memories of children playing and laughing. She couldn't wait to explore.

"What are your plans today?" Jason asked.

"I was just thinking how much I wanted to explore this house with you. It's great. Taylor told me she was born here."

A faint shade of pain darkened Jason's face, and he laid his fork on his plate. "I bought this house thirty-two years ago. It was an extravagant purchase back then, but my wife had taken one look and decided it had to be our home. She loved it. She got to enjoy it for a very short time." He ran a hand over his eyes. "Taylor was born here as her mother and sister died here."

Tiffany bit her lip, knowing she had stumbled upon sacred and painful ground. The silence became oppressive. She cleared her throat. "I'm sorry. I had no idea Taylor had a sister."

"An identical twin. Her name was Tyler. My wife died in childbirth and the first child was weak and died moments later. But Taylor came into the world fighting and very definite that she was going to live." He looked at his hands.

"I'm sorry," Tiffany said again.

"Forest Park and the Central West End area are close by. I'd recommend you start there with your explorations."

"I can't tell you how much I appreciate you letting me stay here. It's probably not going to take too long to find a place."

"Take your time. Donovan moved out a few weeks ago, and the twins left last year for Chicago. I've got six empty bedrooms here. It's way too much for me alone. Shoot, I was thinking about opening a bed-and-breakfast."

"Not a half-bad idea. It seems as if this would be a great area for it."

"I was kidding."

"An alternative is to sell. The house must have had an incredible increase in value since you bought it."

Jason laid his fork down. "Selling Diana's house is out of the question."

Tiffany raised an eyebrow. "Diana was your wife's name." She stated the fact flatly. Didn't he just say that his wife had died thirty years ago?

"Yes, Diana was my wife." Jason turned to put his dish

in the sink and returned to the table with a full cup of coffee. He shook his head a little, as if clearing it of old musty cobwebs. "Let's do all the tourist things today, go to the Riverfront, the Arch, then we can eat out. My treat. You can explore the house and neighborhood anytime."

Tiffany's heart skipped a beat. The man was so fine. She lowered her eyes, feeling flustered. She thought racing pulses and yearnings and physical crushes were over when she'd passed her twenties. No, heck, she knew they were over when she'd married Sidney Eastman. "I'd enjoy that," she murmured.

He grinned at her and touched her hand. The heat between them flared, crackled and sizzled. Tiffany felt like she was having a heart attack, no small concern at forty-seven. The chemistry between them that started in Atlanta was back in full force. But now they weren't on a light-hearted vacation. They were two way-past-grown adults and staying together in a house too large for just two people all alone.

There were seven, count 'em, seven beds in this house. Not to mention several sofas, rugs, stairs and other hard surfaces. The simmering look in Jason's eyes made her bet his thoughts were running along the same lines.

This man could tear the peace of mind she'd regained to shreds with an easy grin. She'd just been through the wringer with a man she'd dated, a man who'd insinuated himself into her life, taken control of her time, emotions, body, and got her hopes up and then beat them down into tatters. She'd be damned if she was going through that again. Next time, whether Jason Cates turned out to be the one or not, she'd be in control.

The air smelled new-spring green, and the breeze that brushed their skins as they strolled through Forest Park was cool and gently caressing. A perfect Sunday afternoon, a day made for lovers to stroll hand in hand in the park.

Tiffany had always thought of herself as a person who was at ease in the company of others and who put others at ease also, but with Jason, she felt she was in junior high. Tongue-tied and awkward, every word issuing out of her mouth was the wrong one.

He was a quiet man, comfortable with silence and obviously the type of man who considered his words very carefully before he uttered them. She glanced at him sideways. His walk was loose and easy, the stride of a physically fit man. His facial features were similarly relaxed and he seemed lost in thought.

A jogger accompanied by a Rottweiler approached. A squirrel flashed across the walk in front of them and the dog surged past the jogger straight toward Tiffany. She gasped and drew close to Jason. He put his arm around her shoulders just as the dog fell back behind its master after a sharp word. The man nodded at Tiffany apologetically as he passed and the dog didn't look at her as it followed its master down the sidewalk.

"Afraid of dogs?" Jason murmured. He didn't take his arm away from around her shoulders, and she felt the warm length of his body next to hers.

"Only real big ones running toward me. I haven't been able to keep from tensing ever since I was bitten as a child."

"Your family didn't have a dog?"

"No. My mother didn't care for dogs."

"I've always had dogs. But the last one, a Labrador, had developed some painful age-related ailments. I had to put her down shortly before Donovan moved out. I haven't had the heart to get a new one with no kids in the house."

Tiffany nodded at his words, but she was too aware of his arm that had slid around her waist, holding her close to him. He held her as if it was wholly natural that their bodies should touch. Their strides matched perfectly.

"My son Dante begged for a dog. I would have been willing to have a small indoor dog, but my ex-husband wouldn't allow a dog in the house."

"Taylor told me about your husband. I'm sorry."

Her jaw tightened. The details surrounding her husband's demise a few years before were never made public. The fact that he shot his son Dante was made to seem like an accident. The fact that he set the fire to their home himself was covered up. The fact that he'd left her bound on the bed to burn alive was never made public. Jason's daughter Taylor rescued her and Sidney burned in the house like he so richly deserved. She had no doubt he was still burning in hell.

"Yes, it was unexpected."

Jason glanced at her, appearing surprised at her tone and choice of words. She couldn't help the dryness in her voice. Congressman Sidney Eastman's death was the best thing that had happened to her and her children.

"How are your kids doing?" he asked.

His question implied that their father's death would have a negative effect on her children, that they grieved his death. Both her children had thrived without the negative influence of their father in their lives. Sidney Eastman may have been a prominent man and a successful politician, but as a husband and a father, he was unmourned and unmissed.

"My kids are doing wonderfully. Better than they ever have. Dante recently married and I have a brand-new grandson named Dante, Jr. Dante works for a law firm in Charlotte, North Carolina. My daughter Jenny is in grad school in Maryland."

"So you're a new grandmother?" Jason said with a grin.

"Yes, and I'm loving it. The only thing that would be better is if I lived in the same city and could see the baby more often." She drew away from Jason to reach into the bag slung over her shoulder. "Want to see pictures?"

"Sure." He nodded toward a bench. They sat under a huge tree and Tiffany pulled out her wallet stuffed full of pictures of her children and her grandson.

Jason looked at each baby picture carefully. When he got to a family portrait of her son Dante and his wife, Celeste, he studied it. "Nice couple. They look happy."

"They are. I was a little worried because Dante met her and married her very quickly thereafter. But she's wonderful and has been a steadying influence. He's had a hard time."

"He has?"

She looked away, wishing she hadn't said anything. "His father was never very supportive of him. I fear it left him with little self-esteem and belief in himself. With his father gone and with his new family, Dante has come into his own. I'm proud of him."

Jason nodded and continued to go through her photographs. He held out a photo to her. "Your daughter? She's quite pretty."

"Jenny. She's doing so much better also. She's majoring in education. She's discovered a real love for teaching and children. We've come to be very close since . . ." Her voice trailed away, sudden memories causing her unexpected pain.

Jason looked at her.

"Her father died," she finished.

"I'm sorry."

"No, it was for the best," she said.

Jason looked taken aback.

She didn't fill in the space left by her statement.

He cleared his throat. "You seem to be doing well. Your life must have changed significantly since you moved from Washington."

"It has, but the changes have all been good. For the first time I'm doing what I want to do and defining who I want to be."

Jason stared at the last picture, a formal family portrait of Tiffany, her late husband and two children. The expressions on their faces were in stark contrast to the more recent photos. They looked like what they had been, a family in pain.

He handed back the pictures to her silently, and she put them away. Memories rose up in Tiffany, and she swallowed, not able to immediately name the emotion. It was more complicated than sadness or grief. Regret, maybe, over her mistakes, over what she had missed. Maybe her children's childhoods would have been different if she had been strong enough to leave her husband sooner than she did ... if she would have gotten help for her own problem ...

Jason took her hand and they entwined their fingers.

"I've always thought that things happen for a reason. We may not understand it at first, but there is always a purpose for what we go through. A lesson, a plan. I didn't understand why Diana died when and how she did. I was so angry. Mad at God and mad at her for leaving me with six kids to raise by myself when we were supposed to raise them as a team in a home full of love.

"When I asked for God's help, He didn't give me an answer why things were the way they were right off, but eventually He gave me strength and renewed my faith. His grace gave me the strength to do what I had to do. I had to do a lot. My children needed so much."

She tightened her fingers around his. When she looked into his eyes, the baggage of their two lifetimes fell away, leaving just them: a man and a woman in the late afternoon sunshine. A shiver ran through her. She didn't want to fully realize how much she wanted this man she barely knew.

He bent his head and his lips touched hers. Softly like a whisper at first. Full of wanting and yearning, tender nibbles and the mere promise of passion. Then desire overtook them and she gave a soft moan as he deepened the kiss and she tasted his hunger. Their tongues intertwined and breathing quickened, their bodies straining toward each other. Suddenly, he raised his head and they were both shaken.

"I'm sorry—" he started to say.

Tiffany touched his lips with her hands. "Don't you dare apologize."

She stood and held out her hand and they walked through the park hand in hand, heading home in comfortable silence.

Chapter 3

Jason rotated his thumb around the center of Tiffany's palm, causing an answering sensation at her very center. New job, new life, she thought. A new affair would be the finishing touch. She'd thought that way once before, after her husband died and she'd moved back to Atlanta from DC. She'd been too eager for love after her miserable, loveless marriage and had gotten burned. There was no reason it should happen again, she told herself. Was there? She squelched the nagging worry that something was wrong with her. Of course there wasn't anything wrong with her.

An affair with this delicious man would be nice. But she wouldn't get her hopes up this time. She remembered the look in his eyes as he assessed her across the bed and again at the breakfast table. Taylor had said her daddy was an upstanding churchgoing man, inflexible, authoritarian and controlling. She'd seen a glimpse of that man last night, but today she'd seen a relaxed, mellow man. A sensitive man who cared enough to draw her out. A man who was interested in her life and what she thought and felt. A man who had loved deeply.

Jason looked at her and Tiffany knew what he was thinking. She knew he wanted her just as much she wanted him. A spell hung between them, the primal attraction between a man and a woman. Was it the pheromones hanging in the air between them? The scent of a mate?

They reached the porch and Jason hesitated at the door as if he were loath to go inside. She didn't want to break the spell between them either. They looked at each other and he pulled her to him. He bent his head and touched her lips softly. A gasp caught in her throat. He deepened the kiss, and his hunger ignited hers.

They both reached for the door simultaneously.

They stumbled through the house and fell on the first cushioned surface they came across, the couch in front of the fireplace. He was on top of her. The weight of his body pressed her into the soft cushions of the couch. He trailed tiny kisses across her jaw line, then returned to devour her mouth.

She arched against him, feeling his hardness pressed against her lower abdomen. Seemingly of their own volition, her legs parted, bringing her feminine softness against him. A purely masculine growl sounded deep in his throat. Slow, deep grind.

He raised and she reached for him, needing, wanting to feel all of him, but he was unbuttoning her blouse and exposing her lacy bra, white against her chocolate skin.

"You're so beautiful," he murmured, nuzzling her throat. He moved downward slowly, tasting and nibbling. His tongue teased in lazy circles over one nipple, then another through the thin fabric of her bra.

Was that a whimper coming from her throat? He reached behind her and with one hand expertly unhooked her bra and eased her blouse off her shoulders, then her bra. It fell to the floor and he lowered his head to her full breasts and teased no more. His tongue worked her nipples into hard peaks and the fire burning between her legs blazed.

His hand rested casually on her knee and moved upward, slipping under the wide opening of her shorts. His finger traced her slit through her damp panties. Then he slipped it under the elastic band and into her soft, warm wetness.

"Yesssss." Her voice was a low exhalation, a hiss.

He expertly caressed the center of where her flame originated and an inferno erupted within her. Her hips rotated with blind, wanton need. She wanted, no, needed to feel this man inside of her, now. Right now. She reached for him.

"Please," she whispered. "Please."

He slid his body up hers with a groan and rotated his hardness between her legs. Oh, God. She reached for his belt and he'd already unbuckled hers. His hands were on her hips, starting to slide her shorts and panties down.

Then he froze. He took a deep breath and withdrew from her, pulling her blouse shut over her breasts. He sat up against the couch and leaned back, his eyes closed, his breath still shuddery.

She struggled to sit up. "What's wrong?"

He opened his eyes slowly and looked at her.

She read his expression. "If you tell me you're sorry again, I'm going to agree," she said.

A wry smile twisted his lips. "I'm not ready," was all he told her. He stood and walked away. In a few moments she heard the door to his bedroom shut and the television come on.

The knife's edge of her arousal faded away. What had she done wrong? She stood on shaky feet and went to her bedroom also. She threw herself across the bed. Now she was getting pissed. She needed to go and demand that they talk. She deserved an explanation. He was old enough to know such sudden sexual rejection would pain her.

She ached inside with unsatisfied need. Right now she

was not up to anything but allowing the bed to support her and help absorb her pain. She closed her eyes and willed the numbing cloak of sleep to cover her.

A little later she woke. She looked at the clock. Nine P.M. She remembered Jason's hands and lips on her and groaned. Was she going to have to find another place to stay? Right now she'd rather run into a pack of rabid Dobermans than him.

But her stomach growled and more imperative needs overrode her immediate desire never to leave the room again. Food, she smelled food. She got up and peeked out her door into the darkened hallway. She heard the TV coming from his bedroom, but no other sound of him stirring within the house. She adjusted her clothes and crept to the kitchen.

He left food out on the stove. She quickly made a plate, got a cola from the refrigerator and went back to her room. She put on the sloppiest pair of sweats she had, picked up the remote by the bedside table, turned on the TV and ate her way through some mindless sitcom and a melodramatic drama. Her mind kept drifting to what happened on the couch. He'd wanted her. It was evident.

So what was wrong? Did he think he'd offend her? Maybe he thought he was taking advantage of her. That might be the reason why he kept wanting to apologize.

That might be what she wanted to think because she wanted Jason Cates so badly she could taste it. She remembered her ex-boyfriend, Dave—and how much she wanted him at the beginning also, and she bit her lower lip. Was she turning into some sort of sex slut as she grew older? All the years she was married, and before that too, sex was secondary in her life, if there at all. Sex was a tool to get what she wanted and to please someone else. It was hardly ever an end unto itself. Sidney Eastman's lovemaking was perfunctory and scheduled. Twice a week, then as the years passed it dropped to once a week and then hardly at all, much to her relief.

She discovered that he'd been cheating on her when her children were still in diapers. Her response was primarily hurt that he didn't feel she was a good enough sexual partner and preferred someone else over her, then anger that he'd allowed another woman to invade their marriage.

Leaving him was out of the question. By then her identity was firmly entrenched as Mrs. Sidney Eastman. If she left him, who would she be?

So in her adult life, sex had been merely the comfort of a body held against her, a human connection. She'd seldom felt desire with the quickened pulse and the craving to have a man fill her until she was free of Sidney and had started dating Dave.

Dave had given her a glimpse of the heights that lovemaking between two people could reach. He'd given her a taste, but not enough to be satisfied. Being with Dave was like climbing a mountain and peeking over. She could imagine what it would feel like to fall off, but she never actually got to jump into orgasm.

Dave had lit a fire in her that she didn't know she could have. She'd wanted someone to grow old with, someone to love her and make love to her. She gave him her all. He rejected her for a younger woman. Had she really faced how much Dave had hurt her? It brought up old painful memories of her late husband's many infidelities. How much she'd craved acceptance and approval, and how he'd spurned the very essence of her, her femininity. Not good enough, not young enough, not sexy enough.

Her salvation would be when she was enough for herself, not some man. When she said it to herself and meant it: Tiffany Eastman is good enough. But the current taste of passion after so many years was sweet. Why deprive herself? She was afraid to dream that it would be love she would get from Jason Cates.

But she craved his body. Her feminine center ached. She needed satisfaction at the memory of his fevered loving. Why had he left so abruptly? What was he afraid of? She could sense the fear rolling off him when he abruptly left.

She could also sense that he was innately a gentleman. He probably thought that casual sex would be an insult to her. He had no idea that that was what she really wanted, zipless sex without all the false hopes and dreams that coupling sometimes held. Satisfaction without expectations and thus the possibility of pain. How could he possibly know?

For once in her life she deserved what she read about in women's magazines, what she heard the women at work talk about. At the rate she was going old age would get her before the big "O" caught up with her.

Unless she let him know. What would happen if she simply went to him? The rules she grew up by said that a woman should never make the first move, especially sexually.

She'd always tried to follow the rules in regard to men, and look what it had gotten her. Heartbreak, disappointment, loneliness, rejection. Screw the rules. Impulsively, Tiffany got up off the bed in a smooth movement. She padded toward Jason's dark bedroom.

Early to bed, early to rise . . . His chest rose and fell with a regular rhythm. She paused and stared at him, afraid, terribly afraid, but her yearning overwhelmed her fear. She moved toward him as if she were drawn. She touched the dark curve of his exposed back with a fingertip. His breathing lightened, became quicker. Her finger trailed downward. A moth's flutter, a butterfly's caress . . .

She slipped between the sheets, her naked body hot and fevered. He groaned and reached for her.

"I need you," she said.

"I want you," he whispered.

He pulled the sheets back and they lay facing each other, silvery moonlight stippling their dark bodies. He had discarded his briefs tonight and slept in the nude. Did some sense tell him that she was coming to him?

He reached out and touched her hip. He eased her on her back and his fingers learned her body, trailing heat over her satiny skin.

She tried to pull him closer, but he resisted.

"No rush; we have all night," he said. He kissed her lips, savoring them slowly. His lips caressed her collarbone, his tongue dipping into the hollow of her neck. She sighed.

"Turn over," he said.

"What do you want to do?" she asked, alarmed.

He grinned. "I want to give you a back rub."

His hands traveled in long, smooth strokes over her muscles, knowing exactly where to linger and to probe. She sighed in pure delight and pleasure.

She felt the touch of his lips on her buttocks and shuddered as his fingers slid between her legs, opening her moistness. His fingers dipped within her and his thumb rotated over her hard bud in a steady, unceasing rhythm.

She whimpered and her hips rotated themselves against the mattress. Control of her body seemed to have passed from her to him as he propelled her with rhythmic pulses, sparkles of tension electrically building.

Suddenly, it stopped as he flipped her over and studied her down there, moving his head closer. She tried to move away, embarrassed. She knew what he wanted to do, but nobody had ever . . .

"I want to taste you," he whispered, holding her firmly.

She froze at the first touch of his tongue, horrified.

"You taste wonderful." He reached for her hands and their fingers intertwined. "Relax," he said. "Please. I love this. I love everything about a woman . . . the scent, the taste, your touch, your pleasure . . ."

He bent his head and groaned in pleasure himself. The

unhurried, steady rhythm of his soft tongue made her feel like warm butter, melting, heating . . . catching flame. Her head arched back and the movements of his lips changed subtly.

"Don't stop. Oh, God, please don't stop."

She was climbing the cliff again and the peak was in sight. She heard animal sounds and wondered if they were from her. He didn't stop the rhythm. Her hips churned and her fingers clawed the sheets. She was almost there, higher . . . and higher . . . and . . . higher . . . and . . .

She fell. Breath caught in her throat, eyes closed, head arched back . . . an exquisite moment stretched out to infinity until spasms of painful pleasure more intense than she'd ever imagined racked her body.

A sob shook her and she drew in her breath harshly as her entire body quivered. No, no, it had never been like this before.

He moved up her body and after protecting them entered her in one movement. She wrapped her legs around his waist and rocked in an instinctive, primordial rhythm. Soft murmurs and moans, whispered whimpers and sighs blended in.

"Go with me again. I'll take you," he said.

And she could hardly credit it, but she could see that mountain again. He filled her all the way up. He held her in precisely the way she would feel him most.

"Take your time. Come with me." His voice caressed her ear.

And she climbed. This was a deep, slow burn, embers fanned delicately that could go out at any moment, or burst into flame. She begged him incoherently, don't stop, please oh, God, don't stop. He reassured her in his gentle voice, and his body urged her upward without ceasing.

And when she fell again, she wondered if she were dying. The epicenter had shifted to deep within her body, and she thought the earthquake would split her apart. Her femininity pulsed and clutched at him. He gave a hoarse groan, shuddered and plunged deeply into her, finally releasing his seed.

They subsided together like the ebbing tide, their limbs wrapped around one another, still joined, sweat drying on their bodies. A feeling of incredible lassitude crept over her. She was completely wrung out, limp, satiated and completed. She closed her eyes.

Chapter 4

The shrill whine of the alarm ripped a jagged edge into Jason's slumber. He groaned and blindly reached to cut it off. A peacefully slumbering warm body was wrapped around his. Mussed sheets and the remnants of sweaty stickiness brought last night's exertions clearly to mind.

Tiffany stirred and felt for the alarm clock. "How do you turn this thing off?" she mumbled. He reached over her and hit the off button and she immediately turned over and went back to sleep.

Jason had a surgeon's long practice of instant waking, and he stood up and stretched his naked body. He headed for the shower feeling numb. He couldn't believe what he had done last night.

The water sluiced over his body, a tad colder than necessary. He considered himself a man with strong moral values. He didn't make love to a woman lightly and never on the spur of the moment. And most of all, never in his wife's house, in his wife's bedroom, for God's sake.

He leaned his head against the cold tiles. It had been

so good. He wanted her so badly that he'd lied to himself. When she slid her hot body next to his, he told himself he was dreaming. He knew better, but it gave him the excuse he needed to reach for her.

He wanted her now. If he didn't need to be at the hospital for his rounds, he'd wake her up and . . . What was he going to do? His lack of control bothered him badly.

Years ago, he'd brought a woman home. He'd kissed her on the couch and they'd progressed to that heated groping stage when he swung around, feeling Diana's eyes on him. His date had looked at him as if he'd lost his mind, and he lost no time getting her out of there.

The experience brought home to him that this was Diana's house and his heart would always be Diana's heart. When she lay dying in his arms he'd whispered that he'd never love anybody but her. He'd begged her not to leave him. He said he'd die too, that she'd take his heart with him. The light had faded from her eyes anyway and a little part of him did die that night.

Of course there had been women. But none for whom he had anywhere close to the feeling he had for Diana. *Not until now,* a voice inside him whispered, and he flinched. He'd let Tiffany into his house. Her second night here they'd made love and it had been incomparable. But was he ready for commitment? Maybe his problem was that he had been too long without a woman. That was what had broken his control. Deep inside he knew that was just an excuse.

He remembered Tiffany's soft moans of ecstasy, her abandonment to pure sexual joy as he pleasured her, and he closed his eyes for a moment. No, she wasn't Diana, but she was so very, very sweet. He couldn't resist her and it was more than sex. Her voice put him in mind of Kathleen Turner's, a husky womanly timbre that sent shivers down his spine. Her scent, womanly and musky scent mixed with spices and flowers, made him tremble. Her confidence and strength mixed with vulnerability turned on every cell in his body. And when she smiled at him . . .

Jason frowned. The desire for her was strong as ever but it was overlaid with something dark within him. Fear. He was more frightened than he could remember. Frightened of a woman holding his heart again. Frightened of wanting that soon turned into need and could all too quickly become loss.

He put his anxiety out of his mind and dressed quickly in the dark and went to the kitchen to make coffee. He glanced at his watch. Six o'clock. He'd better get a move on. After rounds he had a full day of seeing patients.

He returned to the bedroom to wake Tiffany. Today would be her first day at her new job at WomenHelp. When he heard that they were looking for someone new to head up fund-raising, he'd known it would be perfect for Tiffany, an ex-political wife. He turned on the lamp by his side of the bed and stared at her for a while. She was beautiful. Intelligent, responsive and giving—everything he'd ever dreamed of in a woman. "Tiffany," he said softly.

She woke up like a child, stretching and rubbing her eyes. She rolled over to her other side and curled her body up in a tight little ball against the invading light.

"Tiffany," he said, a little louder. "You might want to start getting ready for work. It's past six." She mumbled something and stretched again. She turned over and looked at him and smiled. Pure feline sexiness first thing in the morning. He felt his body responding.

"Thanks for waking me," she said in a husky early morning voice. She rolled off the bed and walked unashamedly to the bathroom. His eyes filled with her lithe nakedness and he almost followed her but caught himself.

He cleared his throat. "I'm off to the hospital."

"Okay," she called from the bathroom.

He paused for a moment, torn inside. Then he turned to go.

Tiffany stared at herself in Jason's bathroom mirror as she listened to his footsteps departing the room. So that was what it felt like. No wonder it seemed that the entire world was obsessed with sex. It was better than good. It had been earth-shattering and painful in its intensity. She couldn't wait to do it again.

But maybe it was a fluke. Maybe she couldn't capture the feeling again. She had become somewhat familiar with that breathless, almost-going-to-fall-off-a-cliff feeling with Dave, her only lover since Sidney died. She just had never fallen before she tumbled down last night. Jason had made her hit the sky so hard she had thought she was dying. She still couldn't believe what she had been missing. She left the bathroom and surveyed the messy bedding. She stripped the sheets quickly and left them in a small pile for the housekeeper that Jason said came every day.

Jason. He was . . . almost perfect. He loved her with the energy and passion of a young man and the experience and soul of one who'd fully lived each one of his fifty-five years. He was all she ever imagined and more. A whisper of fear touched her. The fear of intimacy, of opening up to a man, and the vulnerability that was exposed with it.

She banished the feeling and concentrated on the languid heaviness of a woman who had been thoroughly loved. She felt used and deliciously tired, and for the first time in her life she felt whole. She showered and dressed knowing she finally fit the definition of a sexy woman. Her secret metamorphosis.

When she stood in front of the bathroom mirror wielding her curling iron, there was a new expression on her face, a small smile. Suddenly, she knew Mona Lisa's secret.

A red suit was perfect for her mood and just right to start the first day on a new job. Dynamic, successful, a winner on the brink of new and exciting things. She briskly walked to the car and headed to WomenHelp. Last night had been a good omen. She was on the brink of a new beginning, a new life full of wonderful things she'd never experienced before. She promised herself that.

Tiffany walked into the office and approached the receptionist who was talking on the phone. The woman held up a finger at her and turned away. It sounded like a personal conversation. Tiffany suppressed irritation as long seconds ticked by.

"Can I help you?" the woman finally said.

"I'm Tiffany Eastman," she said.

The woman looked blank. "And?"

"I was supposed to start today. I'll be the new Resource Development Director."

"Oh, you're the fund-raising lady. They weren't sure if you were going to show up. Why don't you have a seat while I find out who's going to handle this."

"Verita Sampson hired me and said I'd report directly to her."

"Ms. Sampson is no longer with us," the receptionist said in tones reserved for the unexpectedly and swiftly departed.

"Oh." Tiffany sank into a chair, her legs weak, her morning ebullience dissipating. She could hardly believe it. Why hadn't Verita called and told her something? Her new boss had seemed so excited when she'd accepted the job. She had said the agency was in desperate need and needed her right away. Now Verita was gone, just like that. Worse, they weren't expecting her.

A sick feeling settled to the pit of Tiffany's stomach.

She'd quit her job in Atlanta on short notice, overturned her life, turned everything upside down to move—

"Ms. Eastman?" A crisp-looking slim blonde, who looked to be in her late forties also, approached and held out her hand. Tiffany stood.

"Please come with me." She turned on her heel with almost a caricature of a military turn.

Tiffany didn't know what to think. She entered a bare and barren office with boxes still waiting to be unpacked sitting in the corners.

"Have a seat." The woman pointed to a chair across from a large, imposing desk. She sat down behind the desk, put on a pair of those glasses that only consisted of the bottom half, and picked up a sheaf of papers. "My name is Moira Linquist. I'm the acting director of this agency."

"I'm quite surprised not to have heard from Verita Sampson about the change," Tiffany said.

"She left abruptly."

Tiffany grew tired of skirting the point, the only point she was truly interested in. "Does the job offer still stand?" she asked.

"Of course. The personnel director tells me you have filled out all the necessary paperwork. You are an employee of WomenHelp this morning and come under our personnel guidelines. We have no reason to discharge you before you've even started the job." The woman gave a thin smile.

Tiffany saw no reason to smile back.

"The transition to this position has consumed my time and attention," the woman continued. "I wasn't sure if Ms. Sampson had gotten in touch with you or not, so I had made no preparations to orient you to our company. My schedule is full for the rest of the day. I'd like you to meet with our personnel director and she can show you around. Maybe you can read some personnel manuals.

Feel free to leave afterward. Be here at seven A.M. sharp tomorrow and I'll meet with you then."

The woman pushed a button on her phone. "Carol, please show Ms. . . ." She looked at her inquiringly.

"Eastman," Tiffany replied, squelching an urge to grit her teeth.

"Please show Ms. Eastman to the personnel office. Bobbie will get you settled in." Then the woman reached for some other papers on her desk, effectively dismissing her.

"Please follow me," Carol said. She was a plump, grandmotherly looking lady with the first friendly smile she'd seen in the place. Tiffany felt like hugging her and maybe indulging in a little cry on her shoulder. But she squared her shoulders and followed her. The day couldn't get anything but better because it couldn't get much worse.

Chapter 5

The personnel director was a young, dark-haired woman with a sweet smile. "It's good to see you again," she said, holding out her hand to Tiffany.

Tiffany searched her mind for the woman's name and was relieved when it came to her tongue. "It's nice to see you again too, Bobbie." This woman had a firm handshake and an uncomplicated, direct look. Maybe she'd let her in on what was going on.

Bobbie picked up two huge binders. "Follow me and I'll get you settled into your office."

She followed her down the hall to a small, dark room on the other end of the suite from Moira's office. There was a desk, empty bookshelves lining a wall and a small table with two uncomfortable-looking chairs. Bobbie dumped the binders on the table. "Personnel manuals, deadly boring reading," she said with a smile. "This used to be Moira's office."

Tiffany was relieved that she had an opening to bring up the topic on her mind. "So Moira's been promoted instead of hired from outside the agency? I was surprised not to find Verita here."

Bobbie's smile faded. "Yes. Moira's worked here ever since the agency opened. Verita started as director a little less than a year ago. We all really liked her."

"I assume you're talking about Verita."

"You assume correctly," Bobbie said.

So possibly the blonde's unfriendly manner and cold demeanor was the result of stress and guardedness. The woman wasn't popular with her staff and she had no idea of the relationship she had with Verita or what Verita had told her.

"I was looking forward to working here. Verita had me all pumped up." She hoped Bobbie would read between the words and comment on what was going on here and what she could expect from this job. If indeed she had a job for long.

"Moira just moved into the position last Friday. It was a great surprise to us all. I'm not surprised that Verita didn't have the opportunity to contact you."

So Verita was fired just last Friday. That explained a lot. "I bet Moira's sudden promotion was a shock to her."

A tiny grimace crossed Bobbie's face. "Not really."

Tiffany looked around at the office, every wall and surface barren and stripped of any personal items, the bookshelves empty. "She sure cleaned out this office thoroughly."

"She sure did," Bobbie agreed. "Moira must have worked through the weekend moving into Verita's office."

There were definite undercurrents to Bobbie's words. Did the employees resent Moira for what happened to Verita?

Tiffany ran a finger over a polished shelf. "What did she do before her promotion?"

"Why, didn't you know? Moira was the Resource Development Director before you."

* * *

The words of the personnel manual blurred before Tiffany's eyes, and she looked at her watch. Bobbie had said she could look over the manuals, then leave. Not surprisingly she was not able to concentrate on the policies and procedures of an agency where she had no idea if her tenure was to be measured in days.

So Verita had hired her to replace Moira and ended up getting fired herself. There was a story in there, and Tiffany was dying to know it. No wonder Moira was so chilly to the woman her predecessor, likely her rival also, had hired to replace her.

Tiffany realized her position at WomenHelp was shaky to say the least. She'd spent long nights in Atlanta worrying about her impulsive decision to move to St. Louis, and right away a worst-case scenario was coming true.

She shrugged and picked up the heavy volumes and placed them on a bookshelf. *Accept the things you cannot change; change the things you can, and have the good sense to know the difference,* she told herself. This was something out of her control. Once she figured out what she was supposed to do, she'd do it to the best of her ability if allowed to do so. She wasn't going to sweat it. Her late husband's premature demise had left her financially independent. Working was a choice, not an imperative.

Right now she had much better things to think about. Jason Cates and the newly discovered delights of the body for one. She swung the handbag over her shoulder and a smile curved her lips. A delicious idea struck her, and instead of sitting in this sterile office staring at incomprehensible and poorly written manuals, she was going to go shopping.

* * *

Jason reached back and rubbed the back of his neck. He finished reviewing tomorrow's surgery schedule with his nurse and he allowed exhaustion to wash over him for a moment. He leaned back in his comfortable leather chair. Time to head home. The thought filled him with an unfamiliar excitement. Tiffany. She was incredible, delicious. Then he remembered that he hadn't gone to church yesterday. It was the first service he'd missed unrelated to his work responsibilities since he didn't know when.

He shifted, not quite knowing what to do with the sudden guilt that struck him. After Diana died he'd been angry with God for taking away the person he cherished most. But the right people always appeared at the right time to show him the way. His faith had grown over the years and it was his center, the balance he relied on to keep from falling.

There were so many who needed him. His patients. His children. Now the kids were gone and the house reverberated with emptiness. He felt at a loss. *What am I going to do,* he'd prayed. The answer came to him, a knowing he'd felt in his bones. *You're going to get up and face another day, do the best you can and be grateful for your blessings. Put one foot in front of another and don't stop walking. Keep treading forward on your journey home to me.*

So that's what he did, but he always had the feeling that God had more in store for him. Then this happened. He rubbed his eyes. He didn't hold to a doctrine of a judgmental God without grace, so it wasn't the act between him and Tiffany that he felt so uncomfortable about. He'd felt tender toward her, protective and caring. He'd sensed a vulnerability about her that touched him. But he should have taken his time with her. They should have built up a relationship first, gotten to know each other better.

Shoulda, coulda, woulda. He knew better than most that those words counted for little. It was what a person did that counted. All the intentions in the world wouldn't make a difference without actions behind them.

He wasn't a saint and he'd been guilty of taking a woman before with only passion between them. But not inside the home he and Diana had shared, in Diana's bedroom. Guilt burdened his heart. He shouldn't have done it. Somehow he'd have to make her understand that he wasn't the sort of man who engaged lightly in physical pleasures. *It was more than physical pleasure between you and that woman and you know it.*

So it was more than physical. He was attracted to her—all of her, mind and soul. But he was too old of a dog for new tricks. For thirty years, women had been pleasant diversions, but none had had influence over him or the way he lived his life or raised his children, although many had tried—and tried hard. He couldn't fathom change at this late stage of his life. Maybe if he'd met her when he'd been thirty. Maybe then.

Why not now, old man? You've shown that you're more than capable of still getting it up . . .

Stop it, Diana! The habit of talking to her in his head was disconcerting, but too ingrained to stop. Diana's voice was a part of him, as much as her house was. Her voice always surprised him when it came. It was irreverent, sharp-tongued and often witty, quite a bit like his daughter Taylor and unlike the misty mental picture of the pious, saintly wife he'd nurtured.

Maybe he and Tiffany should slow down, at least to get to know one another. The passion overtaking them was so quick it gave him no room to catch his breath or to consider his steps. It was as if they were callow adolescents in the first blush of sexual discovery. Every time he stopped to consider what was happening to him, he started to free fall. He tumbled over and over, and the fear made him close his eyes and redirect his attention. He was a mouse in the maze of emotion, and while it felt good, he longed to find his way back to his secure, safe and locked heart of the past thirty years.

The scent of delicious food greeted Jason when he opened the door. Then Tiffany glided into his arms and they closed of their own volition around her lithe body. Her scent assailed him, reminding him of ginger and tropical flowers. Exotic. Sweet. And so hot. He tumbled into her passion helplessly. She lifted her face to his and he touched her lips softly at first, then with increasing hunger.

She pulled away first. "I've made dinner, then I have a surprise for you."

"What—?"

"Don't ask. Then it wouldn't be a surprise, would it?" She smiled at him with a hint of devilment. "I've planned a lovely evening and I want to be in charge, okay? Just relax and let me take care of things."

Tiffany led him into the living room and he was at a loss for words. Soft jazz played in the background and an ice bucket with a bottle of champagne sat on an end table. "Have a seat and relax," she said, handing him a glass. "May I take your tie?" He loosened his tie with a sense of relief and handed it to her. She turned on CNN, with uncanny knowledge that that was what he liked to watch when he got home from work.

"I need to put the finishing touches on dinner. I'll be back in thirty minutes," she said. Then she glided away, leaving him to decompress from the strains of the day alone, which was what he preferred.

He'd steeled himself for emotional talks tonight after their first night of love. He was grateful for the reprieve. He sipped his wine and slipped off his shoes. He could get used to this.

In exactly thirty minutes, she reappeared. "Dinner's on the table." She took his hand and led him to the dining room. The room shone with the soft glow of many scented candles.

She'd prepared a feast of seafood accompanied by simple baked potatoes and a salad. Giant shrimp, fresh oysters on the half shell, a small lobster and crab legs, tender scallops.

"I hope you like seafood." She looked a little nervous.

"I love it," he reassured her quickly.

She woke like a child but she ate like a lady, a queen, he observed as she expertly cracked a lobster claw, removed the tender meat inside and dipped it in butter. She took a bite and her pink tongue darted out to moisten her lower lip. To his astonishment he felt himself harden like he was an eighteen-year-old boy.

"Next Sunday is Mother's Day. What are your plans?" he asked to divert his attention to a safe subject and away from lascivious thoughts.

Tiffany looked surprised. "You're kidding. I completely forgot." Then she frowned. "I wonder why I haven't heard from my kids?"

"I've heard from them."

"You have?"

"This is supposed to be a surprise, but I think surprises of this sort are greatly overrated. They're both flying in Saturday and will stay over to celebrate the day with you."

Tiffany gave a little shriek of delight. "Is Dante bringing the baby?"

"And his wife. The whole family."

She grinned. "This is wonderful news. Lord knows I needed some."

Jason cracked a crab leg. "Tell me what happened at work with your job."

"It's not good. The woman who hired me was fired Friday and replaced by a woman who had the job I was hired for. I gather the plan was that I was to step into her position and she to step out, but apparently it didn't work like that."

Jason whistled under his breath. "I'm sorry. I've known Verita for years. She's very conscientious. Something like this probably hit her hard."

"No doubt."

"So the atmosphere wasn't overly welcoming."

"My new boss makes an iceberg look warm and fuzzy."

"I'm sorry, Tiff. Now, I feel guilty getting you to move all the way up here—"

She waved his words away. "Don't worry. I can get another job if need be or take a little time off. Anyway I was long overdue for a change. I really like St. Louis. It suits me. And . . ." She gave him a meaningful look as her words trailed away. "It's been more than worth it."

He took a sip of water to hide his sudden embarrassment. "Keep me posted about the job."

"I will, but don't worry about it. I'm not going to let it get to me."

"Good. Do I need to get anything for the baby? A crib or something?" he asked.

"Celeste will probably bring everything he needs. She's wonderfully organized. Sweet too. Dante got a treasure when he married her."

They ate for a while in silence. Jason studied her surreptitiously. She was the only woman he could remember besides Diana who didn't have to fill the silent spaces with chatter. She seemed so confident, poised and comfortable with herself. A classy woman.

"I hope you left room for dessert," she said, interrupting his reverie.

"Always," he said, patting his stomach. "But let me help you clear the table first."

"No. Remember you said I was in charge tonight. Let the dishes lie. I'll get to them later. Right now I have something special in mind for dessert." She rose and took his hand, gently beckoning him to follow her.

He couldn't resist. She led him to his bedroom, and the room glowed with the light of at least a hundred scented candles.

He stiffened, not ready for this. But she picked up on his every emotional cue. "I have a bath ready for you. I ran the water very hot so it would be the right temperature."

Candles were also burning on every surface in the bathroom. They smelled deliciously of musk and sandalwood. He wondered when she had gotten them. She touched the water and smiled. "Perfect," she murmured. Then she left him.

He shed his clothes automatically and sank in the water, sighing. This setup wasn't too bad after all. The meal was wonderful and he really liked her as a person. He could get quite used to this sort of pampering. He leaned back and let the jets from the Jacuzzi take away the last bit of his tension.

He wondered what he could do for her in return for this wonderful evening. He pondered the gifts and activities that were supposed to please a woman, jewelry, shopping, dance events and theater tickets. Maybe a fur coat? Jason loved the feel of fur against his skin. But maybe she was one of those animal activists like his daughter Taylor. If not, he'd get her a fur jacket. Dark brown mink would suit her. Then his mind wandered to diamonds and smoky topaz that matched her eyes. After a while he noticed the water was cooling.

When he walked out of the bathroom he gasped at the sight of Tiffany on his bed. She wore a wisp of emerald lace and a wicked smile. He wanted to please her. Right now he wanted it more than anything in the world. He let his towel drop to the floor and reached for her, but she pushed him back against the bed.

"Your turn," she whispered, her voice husky.

Chapter 6

Tiffany reached for a bottle of sandalwood-scented massage oil she'd warmed and set on the bedside table. She drew in her breath at his erect penis. She'd never thought before that the sight of a nude man in his full glory would arouse her like the sight of this one did. He was simply too perfect.

He started to reach for her. "No. Let me," she said. She poured the warm oil over his chest. It pooled a little in the hollow of his neck and ran down to his well-developed pectoral muscles down toward his flat stomach.

"Let me do it," she repeated and for emphasis drew his hands up behind his head. Then she touched him, luxuriating in the sheer pleasure of skin against skin. She closed her eyes and learned his body, the sinew and muscles under his skin, the pulsing warmth.

There was a sexy little growl deep in his throat that emerged when he was aroused. She kissed his belly button, and in incremental inches worked south. When she reached the hard, silky column of his desire, he drew in a quick breath. More oil.

She took her time learning his hard column intimately with her fingertips, and when she lowered her head he was more than ready. She swirled her tongue around him and he groaned. She gauged the level of his arousal expertly, bringing him to the edge.

She pulled back and slid a condom on him slowly and sensually. He moaned and reached for her blindly, murmuring his need. With one quick movement, she impaled herself on him. Her eyes closed in ecstasy as she rotated her hips around him. He filled her up so good, fit inside her perfectly. She heard him say her name, felt his hands on her breasts, on the curves of her body.

Her plans to tease him, to stop and start and take him to the most exquisite finish he'd ever experienced, faded as she melted inside to molten lava. Her world faded to encompass only Jason—his scent, the sounds he made, his burning touch and the inferno he was creating inside her. He grasped her hips as she rode him, her head thrown back, a moan of ecstasy growing in intensity and echoing the feeling building deep inside her.

Don't stop . . . don't stop. Tightening to an exquisite peak within her, so taut, so sharp. It's going to happen . . . again. A gasp. The world stopped. And she exploded. The intensity dwarfed Mount St. Helens, blowing its top and sending her to oblivion or the very heavens.

He was pounding her, drawing the exquisite spasms out and out and out until he stiffened and joined her somewhere beyond reality.

Jason lay wrapped around Tiffany, still inside her heated warmth. A lassitude combined with a warm glow blanketed him. He started to drift into sleep, but she raised her head and kissed his lower lip softly. He curved his arm around her and drew her closer to him. He wanted to stay like this indefinitely with this particular woman in his arms and the cares of the world outside the door.

"It's never been like this for me before," she whispered. Alarm ran through him. Like what? Did he do something wrong? It sure seemed like she enjoyed herself.

"What do you mean?" he asked.

She mumbled something.

"Hmmmm?" he asked.

She looked away and bit her lip. "I've never had an orgasm before," she finally said.

"You're kidding."

"No. It's just been my late husband and one other person, and I never . . ."

"Not even by yourself?"

She hesitated. "No."

"And you did for the first time right now here with me?" he asked, still unbelieving.

She buried her face in his shoulder. "Yes. And yesterday too."

She snuggled deeper into his side like a warm kitten. "Well, I thought I might have had them," she continued. "I wasn't really sure. But what happened to me . . . No. I never had one before."

He didn't know what to say. In that moment he felt as if he was going to explode with pride. As if at forty-seven and with two kids she'd been a virgin offered just to him and him alone. A surge of fierce protectiveness washed through him. "We'll have to make it a habit, won't we?" he said.

She chuckled a sexy contralto ripple. It sent a ripple through him also. "I hope so. I still can't believe what I'd been missing."

"What was wrong before?" He knew it was an awkward question to ask, but he couldn't help himself. How could a man make love to this fabulous woman and not want to please her?

"I don't know. I don't believe the problem was with technical prowess. Maybe it was emotional. My marriage was never very good, not even in the beginning. He started cheating on me after I got pregnant with Dante and started to show. I think he always cheated on me. After the second baby . . . it was real bad. Our marriage was in name only. We had sex only whenever he remembered it. But . . ."

"I get the picture. I'm sorry. You've had it rough."

She propped herself up on an elbow and stared at him. "So have you. Taylor told me you've essentially been without intimate companionship for thirty years although you've had casual girlfriends."

"Taylor talks too much."

"She tells the truth though."

"Yes she does. But for me it was by choice." He waited for the inevitable question about why he'd never remarried, but she surprised him.

"Were you lonely?"

The question shook him. He never thought about being lonely.

He cleared his throat. "Yes, I suppose I was."

"So am I," she said.

The silence stretched out between them as he took in what she'd said. Then she touched her lips to his again and he caught her kiss, took it and made it his own. He lifted his head and rolled her over, putting her hands behind her head like she'd done to him. "Your turn," he said.

The next morning Jason had just finished up a routine surgery when his son Jared paged him. "Dad, we have to talk."

"Sure. Why don't you come out to the house this weekend."

"Before then. It's an emergency."

He'd never heard his unflappable son utter those words before, and alarm tingled through him. "What's up?"

"I can't go through with it. I just can't do it and I have no idea what to do."

Jason knew immediately what he meant. Jared's wedding was scheduled a few weeks hence.

"I'll be getting home on time. Tonight. Dinner at six?" He hoped Tiffany didn't have a full-scale seduction planned like she had yesterday and come to the door wrapped in nothing but Saran Wrap or something. Lord, that woman was hot. He started to warm himself at the memory of her.

Jared agreed and Jason clicked his cellular phone shut. Pre-wedding nerves. He supposed he could relate if memory served him right. As much as he'd been in love with Diana, he had the fantasy of bolting right before the wedding. What was it about weddings and all the folderol associated with them that made women feel like they reached the pinnacle of their lives and made men panic? In his case the ritual solidified the set, unchanging course he'd chosen with Diana. Still, he had panicked that the most important decision of his life could be wrong.

Self-doubt was almost a given when it came to women. In so many ways they were unfathomable and sometimes it was hard to trust mere love. The thought made his mind turn to Tiffany again. He couldn't stop thinking about her. He could hardly credit what she'd said about her limited sexual experience. She'd serviced him like a professional. He suddenly realized his derogatory thought and almost tripped. What was wrong with him?

He hated the lingering feelings of guilt and anxiety, and the tendency to unconsciously devalue a woman who he knew was good. Tiffany was a good woman and he was starting to care deeply about her.

You screwed Tiffany in your wife's bedroom without hesitation. You betrayed Diana's memory. That wasn't Diana's voice, but his own inner fear. He hated the voice that came from the small anxious part of him. It told him that he didn't need this guilt, this anxiety in his life. Sex wasn't worth it. But he hoped Tiffany was.

Chapter 7

"Where did Tiffany disappear to?" Jared asked his father.

"She's in her bedroom with her nose in some book. She said she had a rough week at work and that's how she usually chooses to wind down."

"I wanted to tell her how good I thought dinner was. I'm sorry to hear that her job isn't going well."

"Yes. But she let me know that it's not a necessity for her. She promised to quit if it gets to be too much. And thanks. I cooked the dinner."

"Pretty good, Dad. Are you aiming to impress? I seem to have memories of years of tuna casserole and chili mac and now you're busting loose with chicken cordon bleu?"

"You know you hardheads wouldn't have appreciated my chicken cordon bleu."

"We would have appreciated it more than tuna casserole. So how are you adjusting to a woman in the house after all these years?"

"I'm adjusting just fine, but I thought you came over to talk about your impending nuptials."

Jared started to open his mouth again, but he shut it after a sideways look at his father. Jason knew he was dying to talk about Tiffany. His children were probably buzzing over the fact that he'd finally brought a woman into his home. Well, it was none of their business and he wasn't going to discuss it with them.

"I can't go through with the wedding. I won't. What am I going to do?" Jared interrupted Jason's thoughts and paced the floor looking like he did when he was twelve and struck out when he could have made the winning hit in the championship little league game.

"Marriage is a big step. But most of us get through it," Jason said, sipping a cup of tea.

His son ran his fingers over his close-cropped hair. "The problem is I don't want to get through it. Let me take that a step farther. I'm afraid I'm going to make the worst mistake of my life."

Jason set his cup of tea down. This sounded a bit more serious than he'd thought. "Did you two have a fight?"

Jared ran a hand over his hair. "No."

"So you haven't even talked to her?"

"Not yet. I need to make sure firearms, knives, any sharp implements or missiles are out of her reach before I do."

"That sounds like a good idea," Jason said.

"I'm punking out, aren't I, Dad?"

"Sounds like it to me. I thought I raised a man."

"Thanks for the encouragement and understanding." Jared stood up with an angry motion and his tea spilled across the coffee table.

"I suppose you are a bit too old for me to whip your butt, although you are acting as if it's in order. What's gotten into you?"

Jared sat down again, looking dejected. The first bell of alarm touched Jason. He had been ready to write off Jared's ranting as pre-wedding nerves, but he hadn't seen that expression on his face since he was ten.

"What am I going to do, Dad?" he repeated.

"Tell me what's going on."

"I don't think I love her."

Jason stifled a sigh and went into the kitchen for a roll of paper towels. He handed them to Jared. "What happened? You're not telling me specifics. You loved her when you proposed."

"I thought I did." Jared echoed his father's sigh as he cleaned up the spill. "Benita was the most beautiful woman I'd ever seen, always self-possessed, distant and cool. Since she was white, I just watched her from afar. When I found out she wanted me too—well, the feeling was awesome. We slept together on the first date. Great sex. She dumped her boyfriend and let him know it was because of me."

"This is not a particularly heartwarming story," Jason said with dryness in his voice.

"I know it isn't. That's the point. My girlfriend Stacie had been pressuring me to commit. She wanted a ring; she wanted papers on me. Suddenly, Benita and I were a couple. So I dumped Stacie."

"How romantic," Jason said.

Jared shot a glance at him. "You're making fun of me, aren't you?"

"Only a little."

Jared frowned.

"So what changed your mind?" Jason asked.

"There's something missing."

"And?"

"It's hard to put into words."

"Is there some rule that you can't bring up the subject you want to address with your prospective wife? Or is it the fear of those firearms, knives and other deadly implements I'm starting to believe you might deserve?"

"C'mon Dad. I tried to talk. So you know what she does then?"

"I dare not guess."

"She takes me to bed. She's like a guy under that cool exterior. She likes sports and we talk about issues, ideas and current events. We talk about other people, our work."

Jason stifled the urge to roll his eyes. "I'm not having this discussion with a kid. This isn't the first woman you've been involved with, but it's the first woman you've agreed to marry. You aren't telling me you have had some new revelations about her. I think you suffer from the universal cold feet we men suffer before making a commitment of this magnitude."

"That's what I thought, Dad. But I'm afraid it's more than that. She's different."

"That might have been the reason you wanted to marry her, unlike Tammy, unlike Veronica, unlike Stacie . . ."

"I don't want to spend my life with Benita."

It was Jason's turn to pace now. "You should have realized that a bit sooner than before the wedding dress was fitted. I'm disappointed in you." He frowned at Jared. "Obviously you can't marry someone you don't love. Just be sure that that's the case and it isn't your fear that's making you feel the way you do. I suspect that's what it is."

"Breaking up with Benita right now would be the worst thing I've ever done to another person in my life. I can hardly face it."

"Be a man," Jason roared, and his son flinched. "Take responsibility for your actions. You should be talking to her and not sitting here whining to me. You know what you have to do. My take is that you're scared and you're fishing for an excuse to break it off. You have a history of reluctance to commit . . ."

"You're right, I'm not a kid and I've made a terrible mistake. The mistake started a year ago when I let Stacie go when I started seeing Benita. Last weekend I realized that I should have married Stacie. When our relationship heated up to the point where it had to progress or end, Benita came along and I—"

Jason raised a hand. "I don't want to hear anymore. Go clean up your mess, son. Go do it now. Come to me afterward. I'm willing to help you in any way I can. We'll figure this out together. But now you need to go do what you have to do."

Jared started to say something but shook his head instead. He stood and walked out the door.

Jason stared after him. He was disappointed with his son. He thought he'd raised a man who knew his own mind. Although being confused about women was understandable.

Jason sat back on the couch and picked up the remote, unseeingly flipping channels. He could empathize with his son being swept away by a sexually overcharged woman more than he let on.

He started to try to put his finger on what was bothering him, but his mind skittered away and turned to the replay of tonight's baseball game. There was one emotion that he'd accused his son of that he couldn't run from. Fear. He feared emotional upheaval, his life changing, and irrevocable decisions. What did she want from him? It had to be more than just sex. With a woman it always was. The most important question was what did he want from her? He knew it was more than sex, but he didn't know exactly what. Whatever it was, it heralded change and that profoundly unsettled him.

Jared drove home from his father's house feeling upset and depressed. His father's words rang in his ears. "Be a man!"

The bad part was that his dad was right. He should have

talked to Benita weeks ago. But every time he tried to steer the conversation in that direction, she resisted. The few times he tried to voice his doubts, she'd immediately accused him of having cold feet because of their racial differences. That quickly shut him up.

She'd talked the race thing to death, going over every permutation and possibility of the prejudice they and their children were sure to face. It didn't make it any easier that her father was the very incarnation of David Duke. It was her favorite topic. He knew it had to be addressed, but he was beyond sick of it.

What was up with the woman? He wondered why she wanted to marry him. Besides the sex, she didn't seem to have much respect for him. He'd shrugged it off before, thinking she was simply a domineering type of woman. The underlying veneer of her personality structure was cold and take-charge. It made her occasional warmth that much more exciting.

He flipped open the cellular phone and called Benita's place. The phone rang until her answering machine picked up. Then he remembered that she was working tonight. He made a right almost without thinking and turned to drive in the other direction. His fingers punched out a number on the phone. Stacie answered on the first ring.

"It's me, Jared. Can we talk?"

"What about?"

"Us. I want to talk about us."

There was a pause. "Okay," she said.

"I'm on my way."

Tiffany looked at her watch. It was after ten and she'd finished her book. Jason was still in the den. She assumed he was talking with his son. Jared was obviously very worried about something. When they'd eaten dinner, the atmosphere had been tense with unsaid things. They'd excused themselves and disappeared into the den before she'd even finished eating.

She wondered what to do. Although she and Jason had shared intimacies, going to sleep in his bed without his knowledge or consent seemed a violation of his boundaries. But after being bruised and battered at work today, she needed him to hold her. She ached for the comfort of his arms.

They'd been together two times and each time she'd gone to him. She ought to give him a chance to reciprocate. She got up and ran a tub full of water. Sinking down into water as hot as she could stand it, she listened for his footfalls, the tap of his hand at his door. She waited. The bath water cooled. Reluctantly she stood. She put on a sexy piece of lingerie she'd recently purchased. He was coming. Surely he would.

She lay on the bed with a book. Her eyes got heavier each second and the words blurred in front of her eyes. She turned off the light. She'd catch a few winks before he came to wake her.

"Tiffany?" he whispered, his voice slipping through her sleep and melting in her ears like butter. She rolled over and opened her eyes. He was a dark gray shape over her and she smelled the sweet scent of his breath. He slid under the covers and took her in his arms. She relaxed against the warmth of his skin and the security of his enfolding arms. Yes. This was what she wanted.

"I'm sorry to wake you," he said.

There was a certain tension in his body she sensed. He needed to talk. "That's okay. How did your talk go with your son?"

"He wants to break off his engagement."

"Oh, no. Isn't he getting married in Atlanta pretty soon?"

"He's got cold feet. I fear this isn't just a chill either. They're blocks of ice."

"Still, that's pretty normal. Broken engagements are easier to get over than a broken marriage. Why are you so bothered?"

Jason rolled on his back and rubbed his eyes. "I'm disappointed in him. He's a thirty-five-year-old man. He won't settle down and this isn't the first girl he's hurt. I hoped I'd raised sons who were capable of good relationships with women. Maybe if they'd had a mother—"

"Jason, stop it. You are a wonderful father. I know how it is to feel responsible for who your kids turn out to be, but at a certain point you have to accept that you did the best you could."

"And turn their sorry butts over into God's care and keeping?"

Tiffany chuckled. "Something like that. But I know exactly where you're coming from. I had many a sleepless night over my grown children, especially Jenny. Thank God she's doing all right now, and Dante has always been a pleasure. Not a peep of trouble out of him."

"I bet he's a mama's boy."

Tiffany hit him in the shoulder. "Of course my baby is a mama's boy, but not the way you think. He's all man."

"I thought it would be so because who could help but adore such a woman as yourself. If you were my mama, why I'd—"

"Still be breastfeeding?"

"Good idea."

"You're a sick man."

Then Jason's mouth was full and Tiffany's giggles soon turned into moans of pleasure.

The office was open but the receptionist's desk was empty. Tiffany went into her office and sipped the Starbucks coffee she'd bought on the way to work. She stared out the window at the city stirring in the early morning light. Two minutes to seven.

At exactly seven she rapped lightly on Moira's door.

"Come in."

Tiffany stepped inside and closed the door behind her. Moira sat behind her desk with a steaming mug of coffee and a mouthwatering muffin in front of her. In the morning light, Tiffany could see the network of lines around her eyes. She wasn't as young as she first had seemed. Probably around her age, although, being a thin-skinned blonde, she could be younger.

"Have a seat." Moira took a bite of the muffin. "I stopped at the Saint Louis Bread Company and picked up a couple. Would you like one?"

Tiffany started to demur and reconsidered. "Thank you."

"Look in the bag on the table beside you. There's a cup of coffee in there. Hazelnut flavored, if you like that kind."

Tiffany set the muffin and coffee on the edge of Moira's desk. "Do you mind?"

"Of course not."

The silence was almost companionable as Tiffany spread real butter, softened to a perfect consistency on the muffin bursting with shredded carrots, walnuts and raisins. She bit into it and closed her eyes. Heavenly.

"Good stuff, huh?"

"Excellent." She sat back and waited for Moira to lob the ball back to her.

"You've been away from Washington how long? A couple years? How are you adjusting?" she asked.

"Very well, thank you."

"It must be a shock entering the working world after so many years of only being a politician's wife."

"Who says that wasn't work?"

Moira drew in a breath, clearly surprised. She chuckled.

"Who, indeed? I never cared for your husband's politics. Conservative Republicanism isn't my cup of tea."

"Mine neither."

Moira's eyes widened. "Really? I had no idea that was allowed."

"Differing from my late husband's politics? It probably would have been quite awkward if I had cared about politics one way or another when I was married to him. After he died I reevaluated my life and defined myself more fully than I ever had before. In the process I burned my Republican Party membership card. I'm an Independent now and proud of it."

Moira looked at her with a newly assessing glance. "I'm happy to hear that. To be honest, I wasn't happy when I heard that Verita had hired someone to replace me. I had no idea I was to be let go when I found out. I was even more dismayed to hear it was Tiffany Eastman, wife of the late leader of conservative, bourgeois African Americans. I'd always thought of him as corrupt and a sellout to the very people he claimed to serve."

"Frank words. Let me be as frank. What happened to Verita?"

"She overreached her grasp. The board fired her Friday when some of the agency's financial inconsistencies came to light."

"And how did these inconsistencies come into the light of day?" Tiffany inquired.

Moira leaned back in her chair. "You've been around the block. You can guess what I did."

"I see." Tiffany took another bite of muffin and chased it with the coffee. "My primary concern is if I have a job here."

"You don't need to work, do you?"

"That's not your concern."

"I agree. I simply would like to know your motive for coming to us."

"I like the agency. It has a wonderful reputation and I believe in the cause of helping women achieve independence and self-sufficiency through creative means. Fundraising is what I've done for years in one capacity or another for my late husband and others. I have connections. Finally, I want to work. Shopping and giving parties can be tedious occupations after a while."

Moira nodded. "Fair enough." She stood. "I'll have Carol bring my old files and materials over to you to go over and familiarize yourself with the job. She'll also sign you up for a grant-writing workshop that's starting in a few days." She stood and extended a hand. "Welcome to our team."

There was a definite thaw to her voice and a gleam of respect in Moira's smile. Tiffany grasped her hand and an exchange of feminine understanding ran between them. They were going to be friends.

Chapter 8

Standing beside Harry, the surgeon who was assisting him, Jason scrubbed in silence. They each had an unspoken rule about talking in the early morning. Neither particularly believed in it unless it was absolutely necessary. His first case was a fairly routine coronary arterial bypass graft, CABG for short.

The only thing the slightest bit unusual about it was that it was the second one he'd done on a relatively young woman. Lydia Hodgson was only fifty and he'd done her first one nine years before. She had a history of severe coronary disease. Both her parents had died before they'd reached fifty. He'd been following her for twenty years and she was a near-perfect patient, compliant and successfully making every lifestyle change he'd recommended. She was a vegetarian, only eating fish and the very occasional chicken breast. She exercised regularly and had a loving and supportive family. Yet, Lydia's arteries had become clogged to the extent that the medicinal intervention he greatly preferred hadn't been enough. He reluctantly suggested another surgery. "Life is important to me," she'd said. "I'll do whatever it takes. I'm just getting started, Doc," she'd said with a wink.

It was an hour into the surgery. The soothing sounds of Mendelssohn in the background blended with the whoosh and beeps of the machinery. After so many years he'd never gotten accustomed to the wonder of the heart-lung machine. Drugs are given to prevent the blood from clotting, then it's shunted into a machine that cools the blood, thus the body. The heart is stopped, silent.

"I wonder what's it's like to be dead?" a patient once asked him. None of the many surgical patients whose hearts had been stopped and their bodies cooled had ever commented about it once they'd been revived. Technically, of course, they weren't dead. A machine oxygenated and circulated their blood to their brain and body tissues. But there was something disquieting about a silent heart.

The repair proceeded uneventfully as planned. The electric current to restart the heart was given, and Jason felt the customary thrill he always felt when the muscle started its rhythm of life again. Sometimes he felt as if his surgical skills and techniques were but an act of faith. At best he was only a conduit of the will and power of God. *Thy will be done,* he'd pray, and turn the outcome over into His care and keeping.

"Heads up, guys," the anesthesiologist said. "We're getting some dysrhythmia." Jason frowned and turned his head to study the strip that the anesthesiologist held up for him.

Alarms started beeping. "Oh, hell," the anesthesiologist said.

Sweat dripped down Jason's forehead as he snapped out orders for the appropriate drugs. Tense seconds went by. The drugs weren't working. He merely had to glance toward the piece of machinery in the corner of the room, which would take over the work of the heart, and the circulating nurse nodded.

Lydia skated that fine line between maintaining the blood flow that carried the precious oxygen to her brain, and kidney shutdown. *This can't be happening,* he thought as he inserted the pump. The machine might stabilize her. But for only a while. She couldn't live on the machine. If her heart muscle was damaged beyond repair, she would die anyway.

"SVR is falling." His scrub nurse, Althea, had prepared the dopamine before he could voice the order.

An alarm shrieked. Her heart muscle shivered and quaked and finally lay still despite all the fancy cardiac drugs and machinery modern medicine had to offer. They'd done all they could. A few moments in time and Lydia was gone. *Thy will be done.*

"Close her up for me, Harry," he whispered. Althea trailed him with tears running down her face.

He told the circulating nurse to ask the family to wait in the separate waiting room, the room that existed to afford privacy while the family was given news. Sometimes good, more often the worst.

Althea wiped her eyes and tried to compose herself. He walked in with a flash of déjà vu. The heavy waiting and almost palpable tension. They always looked into his face. Always.

Jason looked at Lydia's husband and he looked away and buried his face in his hands. He didn't want to hear what Jason didn't want to say.

"Oh God, no. Oh, God. No. Noooo." The keening from her daughters had started and Lydia's son turned his face to the wall. Jason cleared his throat. What could he say? He knew the words, had uttered them countless times. Why weren't they getting past his throat?

"I'm sorry. We did all we could do, but—"

The daughter's keening rose to a scream, cutting off his

words. Her baby's cry joined hers, terrified. A nurse rushed in to take the baby.

Jason felt old and unbearably tired. Sick with grief himself, he had nothing left to give. He met Althea's eyes and observed her imperceptible nod. She'd put her own grief aside and taken care of this family. He'd have to finish. They always needed the details to hold on to. They grasped them, trying to understand the unfathomable. He felt obligated to list exactly what happened and what they did—each and every lifesaving measure so routine that it was automatic. *We did all we could. Really we did.* So why did he still feel guilty? Or was it a deep burn of anger buried so deeply he could barely detect it? *Thy will be done?* Why now? Why her?

Finally it was over. He dropped a heavy hand to Lydia's husband's shoulder as he passed out of the door. They had shared a lifetime together. He knew the past twenty years of their ups and downs and how much they'd looked toward this time and growing old together.

"We did all we could, but . . . she's gone." Such cold words to end a lifetime of love and care.

There was another surgery on his roster. He went in and started scrubbing. Harry touched his shoulder. "You want me to cover for you, buddy? I know it was rough."

Jason shook his head. "Thanks, but I got it."

His patients counted on him, put their lives in his hands. He continued scrubbing and stuffed his grief down to that little place in his heart where it always went.

Much later, after the surgeries were done for the day, Althea touched his shoulder. "These things happen, Jason," she said. "You know there was nothing more you could have done."

He nodded. These things happen. They didn't happen often, but he had had to walk into that little room far too often for his own comfort lately. Usually it wasn't like Lydia. Usually death, even when sudden, was somewhat expected.

The patient was so sick that the operation being done was a long shot. Or it was an emergency surgery where they were attempting to reclaim a heart, the life of which had already almost drained away. In those cases they were steeled mentally somewhat for the eventuality of death. He never played Mendelssohn at those times, but labored in silence.

He'd done all he could. Always. But this time all he could wasn't enough. He walked into the hospital shower and allowed tears to fall freely. He'd come to the conclusion years ago that unshed tears subtracted years from a person's life. But similarly, long years of cultural conditioning prevented his tears from being absorbed and soothed by another person. He always cried alone in the shower, his only company the keen pain of loneliness.

He remembered that last week he'd just finished his examination of her and a chart had slipped from the counter behind him. He'd turned and bent to pick it up. "Doc, I know life isn't forever, especially with my disease. I could die in the next moment. So I'm going to enjoy this one all I can. And this is one nice view. Damn, you're a fine man. If I wasn't happily married, you'd be in a heap of trouble . . ."

He'd swung around, his face warming, and laughed along with her.

When he told her of the extent that her arterial disease had progressed since her last bypass, she'd tensed and relaxed slightly. "I did everything you told me and read up some more so I could do more. Every time something tempted me—a piece of chocolate cake or barbecue, or finishing a juicy romance novel instead of exercising—I'd think of my kids, and doing what I needed to do would get easier."

She looked at him out of the corner of her eye. "Sometimes we don't get what we want, huh? If it wasn't for what

I did and that surgery I had I'd probably have been dead years ago.''

He hesitated and then nodded. ''So this time was a gift and look what I did with it! I raised my kids, I've seen my grandchildren. I've learned the only thing that really counts in life are the people you share it with. Go ahead and do the surgery, Doc. Do the best you can, but what will be, will be. It's past my time and God might just want me to come home.''

Had she known?

''The only thing that matters in life is the people you share it with,'' she'd said.

God had taken away his Diana before she could see her children grown and having kids of their own. He'd been so lonely, so very lonely. A flash of Tiffany's face. Why was he so scared? ''Every person who comes into your life is there for a purpose,'' Lydia had said once.

He was fifty-five years old and his kids were gone and he was alone. He remembered that Lydia had grasped his hand after her decision. ''I don't want to have the surgery. I remember the pain of the last one and this one scares me down to my bones. I'd try to put it off or try some of those new things you told me about, except the chest pain is getting worse, much worse, and sometimes I see the old reaper out of the corner of my eye. It's Charlie. He needs me. He's given me so much care and love. I have to do it for him. He told me he couldn't imagine having to live without me.'' Lydia bit her lip and looked off into the distance. ''One day I think he will and he's a strong enough man to manage it. But God willing, that day won't be soon.''

Jason turned off the shower with a sense of quiet realization. He was happy Tiffany would be there when he got home. It had only been a few weeks and already he didn't want to go home to an empty house. He'd just picked up his shirt to dress when his beeper went off. An emergency surgery he'd been asked to consult on. A favor called in that he'd owed on.

He reached for a clean scrub top instead and called the house to leave a message that he'd be home late.

"How's the job going?" Moira asked. Tiffany looked up from her desk.

"It's going fine. Come on in."

Moira sank in a chair next to Tiffany and stretched and sighed. "Sometimes I have to escape my office for a while. I feel like I'm on display and I don't dare let my persona drop for an instant."

"Which one? The hard-as-nails bitch, the bitch with the balls or that frosty heifer I met when I first got here?" Tiffany asked.

Moira chuckled. "All of those, I suppose. I am somewhat enamored of that ballsy bitch though. She's gotten me pretty far in life."

"I don't doubt it."

"Seriously, how are things going? Like your job yet?" Moira asked.

"In fact, I do. Especially with the autonomy you've given me."

"You could look at it as rope to hang yourself."

"I suppose I could if there were a possibility of that ever happening."

Moira grinned at her. "You got some balls yourself, lady." She sobered. "I've heard through the grapevine the inside story of what happened to you in Washington. You are one strong black woman."

Tiffany's answering smile faded. "You have me mistaken for someone else. The strong black woman is dead."

"Excuse me?"

"Yes, that mythical woman finally passed away. Dead of

loneliness, overwork, frustration, dashed hopes and broken dreams. May she rest in peace.''

"Have I offended you in any way?" Moira looked worried.

"Not at all. I just wanted to let you know that the woman you referred to no longer exists, if she ever did. What's left is simply a woman, a black woman who rises to the occasion of difficulties in her life like she always has. But she no longer is expected to be strong only by virtue of the color of her skin. She is entitled to the support and love every woman deserves."

"My, my. I don't disagree with you, but what's up with you this morning, Tiffany? Your soapbox is mighty high."

"Sorry. I know you didn't mean anything by the statement, but that 'strong black woman' thing just rubs me the wrong way. I've always needed what every other woman does and suffered for the lack of it the same way every woman does too. I've never seen the point in garnering kudos for going through hell. If that's so, it's not only black women who've earned them."

Moira looked at her hands. "True. I've earned my share in this life."

She glanced up at Tiffany out of the corner of her eye. "How's it going with that man you're staying with? I've heard stories about the fine but impossible-to-pin-down surgeon, Jason Cates. He causes quite a titter in circles of St. Louis single women. I hear there's a jackpot for you to claim somewhere for being the first woman who gets cozy in his house."

"Goodness. So the word is out about me?"

"Not from me, but you'd be surprised at the number of women keeping tabs on Dr. Cates."

Tiffany sighed. "He's all that, Moira, but he's still a man. A man who has been a bachelor for thirty years."

"Giving you fits, huh?"

"He's wonderful. The type of man you could lose your

mind over. But I've done that once and I'm not about to do it again."

"Afraid?"

"Terrified."

"I can imagine how it would be. But be grateful you have company on those long, lonely nights."

"You're an attractive woman. I can't believe you have a tough time getting company yourself," Tiffany said.

A wry looked crossed Moira's face. "I'm forty-four years old. Good company isn't easy to find."

"You haven't been divorced long, have you?"

"Two years. The marriage wasn't much but at least he was company."

"Has he remarried?" Tiffany could see in Moira's eyes and voice remnants of the pain of being abandoned by the man for whom she'd sacrificed her youth. It wasn't readily identifiable except by another woman who had been through it herself.

"Yes. The ink on the divorce papers was barely dry. She's thirty-two."

"Trophy?"

"You know it."

"I do. I never had to worry too much about being abandoned because I was a political wife, but the creeping and sneaking gets to you after a while, you know?"

"I know." Moira struggled up. "I'd better get back." She dropped a hand on Tiffany's shoulder. "Better luck this time."

"You too."

Tiffany gazed into the distance for a while after Moira left. She didn't quite know how they had become close so quickly, but there was a basic honesty and earthiness about Moira she liked. They'd clicked and their conversations always meandered to the intimate things that mattered to women: connections, relationships and feelings.

Despite their differences, she knew in her heart that

Moira was a friend, and she trusted her. She worried about her, though. Moira had few allies in the office and no friends after her protracted battle with the popular Verita. Her job meant a lot to Moira and bespoke of an emptiness in her life. Sometimes it seemed like she hated to go home to her empty house. She had one daughter at an East Coast university. She didn't have the comfort and the distraction of young women like Kara and Taylor, which Tiffany had had thrust into her life when Sidney died. All Tiffany could do was to be a friend to her. And to be honest, right now she needed Moira as much as Moira needed her.

Tiffany used the garage door opener that Jason had given her and pulled her car in. Disappointed, she noticed Jason wasn't home yet. She'd hoped to see him. She banished her disappointment as she let herself into the house. A blinking five on the answering machine. She hoped at least some of the five messages were for her.

She missed . . . well she missed everything. Her children, her friends, her life. This move was taking more out of her than she cared to admit. She pressed the buttons to listen to the messages and smiled to herself when she heard her friend and Jason's daughter Taylor's cheery voice. "Tiffany! I miss you. Call and tell me what's going on. All hell has broken loose with my job here in Atlanta. Literally. Call me, okay? Oh, yeah. Hi Dad!"

"Mom, it's Jenny. Call me as soon as you get in."

"This message is for Tiffany Eastman," her son's voice said. "Mom, happy Mother's Day! Give me a call. Hope you've settled in well."

"Tiffany. You all right? I just wanted to check since I hadn't heard from you," Sidney's daughter Kara said.

"Tiffany? Jason. I'm still in surgery. I won't be home until late. Take care and don't wait up."

She grinned. Five messages and every single one for her. And she'd completely forgotten about Mother's Day. She called Dante back first. His wife answered the phone.

"Celeste, this is Tiffany. How are you?" Genuine pleasure infused her voice. She cared about the sweet girl that Dante had been so fortunate to marry. "How's my grandbaby?"

"He's doing just fine. Getting heavier by the minute."

"Getting fatter, hmmmm? Let me talk to him."

She listened to the baby cooing and gurgling and laughed back at him in delight. Celeste took the phone away from the baby too soon; she could have listened to Dante Jr.'s baby noises for an hour.

"It's going to be so great to see you. It's been too long," Celeste said.

"I agree with that, but when are you going to see me?"

"Dante didn't get hold of you? We're flying down for Mother's Day, all of us. Jenny's coming too. It's supposed to be a surprise, but oh, well."

"That's wonderful!"

"Dante cleared it with Jason. In fact, I think it was his idea. We were going to stay in a hotel."

"I can't think of a better Mother's Day present."

After Tiffany returned all the calls to her children and children-in-spirit like Taylor, and her stepdaughter Kara, Tiffany hung up the phone, feeling excited. She was going to see her children. She'd missed them terribly ever since they split up after Sidney died. After she returned to her hometown, Atlanta, Dante took a job in Miami and Jenny went on to graduate school in Maryland.

This was the first time they'd be together since little Dante was born and they had all gotten together to celebrate his arrival at the hospital. It would be a great weekend, she thought as she went to change her clothes and then go find something to eat.

* * *

Stacie opened her door with a slight frown on her pretty brown face. "What do I owe this rather late visit to, Mr. Engaged Jared Cates?" But she stood aside to allow him entrance as she uttered the somewhat bitter words.

Jared walked into her familiar apartment. His primary emotion was . . . relief. Relief with a touch of shame. He was about to take a step that would irrevocably break his engagement. "I'm not going to be engaged much longer. I'm breaking up with my fiancée," he said.

Stacie sank into a chair and picked up the remote to turn off the television. He sat on the couch adjacent to her.

"I notice your statement refers to the future and you still referred to the white woman as your fiancée," she said.

He sighed, noticing that she had not offered him a seat or anything to drink. He always thought what irked Stacie most was not merely being dumped by him, but being dumped for a white woman. The relief he felt lessened. "I'm sorry that things turned out like they did. I made a mistake."

"I agree that you did make a mistake and you are sorry." She folded her arms across her chest and glared at him. "So what do you want?"

He shook his head and clasped his hands together looking at his feet. "I don't really know, Stacie. I was feeling pretty bad. I told my father that I didn't want to go through with the marriage and he let me have it. I guess I needed someone to talk to. I guess I didn't want to go home to an empty apartment."

Silence. Too long a silence. He looked up at her and her face was buried in a pillow, her shoulders shaking uncontrollably. Was she crying? Oh God, he hated it when women cried. Especially over him. She lifted her head and he saw she was laughing. The tears streaming down her face were tears of mirth. He was confused.

"Man, are you a piece of work. First, after two years together you leave me for some white woman with nary a word of explanation. Then you show up at my doorstep at the first sign of trouble girlfriend gives you, saying you want to talk. You don't want to be alone."

She stood and suddenly all signs of mirth drained from her face. "I was so surprised to hear from you, I must admit I was curious at what you had to say to me. Is that it? You just want me to soothe your emotional pains?"

All he could do was nod. He became alarmed as Stacie's fists clenched and a look like she was in some sort of pain came over her face. My goodness. What was wrong with her? he wondered.

"Get the hell out of my house," she suddenly yelled, causing him to flinch. "You sure didn't give a damn about my emotional pain when you dissed me for that witch." Stacie swung open the door. "Lord forgive me, the man made me cuss," she muttered to herself.

Jared was too astounded to move from his place on the couch. In all the time they were together, he'd never heard Stacie utter a word of what she termed bad language. "You must want me to hurt you. Get out!" she shrieked at him.

He got up and moved out the door and it slammed behind him so hard the doorjamb shuddered. He saw neighbors peeking out into the hallway. He smiled lamely at them and took a deep breath and knocked on Stacie's door again.

"Oh, I see," he heard her yell through the door. "I'm supposed to call 9-1-1 and get a restraining order on your sorry ass."

The little old lady to the left cleared her throat, and he turned and waved at all the doors up and down the hall that were cracked open to enjoy the spectacle. "Everything is all right, folks. You can go on in now." He turned back to Stacie's door. "Please don't call 9-1-1. Let me in. Please. I'm begging to talk to you. I'm sorry. I was wrong."

"That's right, young man, get down on those knees!" he heard a voice yell from down the hall.

"Pleeeeze, Stacie, let me in now."

"Naw, don't let him in, girl," another voice yelled.

"Why should I? What do you have to say to me?" Stacie demanded through the door.

"I made a mistake. I said I'm breaking off my engagement."

"Too bad you didn't think about the mistake you made when you left me for that white woman."

"I know that's right," came a male voice.

"I hurt you. I was stupid. I'll make it up. I promise," he said. "Just let me in."

"How do you propose to make it up to me?"

"Yeah, honey, make him put his money where his mouth is."

He shot an evil glance down the hall.

"What do you want me to do? I'll do anything," he said, feeling desperate and trapped. He couldn't just walk away. She had to let him in.

"I don't see a ring on *my* finger," Stacie called.

A chorus of whoops and catcalls broke out to his left.

"You want a ring?" he croaked.

"Jared, we were on the verge when you went off and dumped me for that . . ."

He raised his arms and leaned against the door, as if the police were getting ready to frisk him before they slapped on the cuffs and hauled him off to jail.

"Okay," he said, his eyes closed.

The door opened suddenly and he fell into the apartment. He rolled on the floor and listened to the applause in the hallway and looked up into Stacie's triumphant eyes.

"Heaven help me," he said.

Chapter 9

Tiffany instantly recognized the touch along her back. Jason had come to her. His hand reached down to the nude curve of her hip and dipped in the soft swell of her belly. He groaned and stretched his body along hers. "Tiffany," he whispered.

She opened for him like a flower, already wet and ready, and he slipped inside her. They made love like a slow dance to Mozart. Regular in its rhythms, intricate in its nuances of note and form. Long, easy and very, very slow.

He was exquisitely tender. "Ahhhh, it feels so good to be inside you." His words were followed by the touch of his mouth and the mere whisper of a kiss. When she tried to speed up the rhythm to her own frantic passion, he resisted. "We have all night," he said.

He moved his body within hers with long, deep, tireless strokes that she knew with a certainty wouldn't stop. She matched him, luxuriating in the feel of him within her. A slow burn ignited inside, surprising her. She'd never experienced it with just the feel of a man's body on hers as he moved within her in the most intimate caress possible.

Slow and steady, he stoked her fire down deep. Glowing embers fanned by a regular rhythm. She felt every inch of him enveloped in her warm, slick sheath. His murmurs about the delights of her body mixed with the beat of his heart against hers.

No, don't ever stop. A fine sheen of sweat covered both their bodies. She strained to him and he kissed her, deep and tender, yearning and sweet, joined at two points.

And with a gasp, she burst into unexpected flames. The inferno caught her from deep within and burned longer and more fiercely than it ever had before. She would have screamed if she could breathe. He jerked and bucked inside her with his own ecstasy and it drew her own spasms out to an almost unbearable length.

Afterward, they lay entwined, taking deep draws of each other's breath. He propped himself up on an elbow and touched her cheek. "The missionary position never felt so good before."

She chuckled. "It makes me happy that you came to me."

He didn't answer for a moment. "I needed you," he said.

She could barely hear him, but she still caught the undercurrents of anxiety in his voice. They parted and the cool air felt delicious on Tiffany's overheated body. "What happened today?" she asked, trying to sound casual, light.

"My patient died. No, she was more than that. My friend died. A fifty-year-old woman."

"My God. I'm sorry."

"Her name was Lydia. She loved her life and she made a point of living every moment fully. She had more of a life than most ninety-year-olds."

Tiffany realized that any more words would be superfluous. She rubbed a finger across his cheek, feeling the coarse stubble just breaking free of his skin, smelling the masculine musk of him, earthy and sweet. She didn't want to face just how much she loved this man. It was too soon.

"I missed you," he said, and she swallowed a sob of joy and pain. With so much caring came so much fear. He had the power to hurt her as much as he had to please her.

"I missed you too," she whispered.

He cradled her in his arms and soon his breathing deepened in sleep. She stayed awake for a while, savoring the feel of his body next to hers.

"Tiff, I left my mug of coffee on the counter. Could you go and get it?" Jason called from his Jeep.

"Sure, hon." They'd graduated to casual endearments. The days had passed in a haze of work and idyllic lovemaking. They had gotten to know one another better, adjusting to their habits and engaging in light conversation. But as Tiffany's attachment and pleasure in Jason grew, so did her anxiety. She sensed the same in him.

Oh, they could talk about intimate details of their pasts, their children and their histories, but for some reason they were reluctant to talk about what mattered, their feelings. Especially their feelings for each other. If Jason was like most men, Tiffany doubted if he even knew exactly how he felt. And like in most new relationships, the unspoken taboo was there against asking directly what you most wanted to know. *How do you feel about me? Do you think I'm good enough for you? How far do you want this to go?*

She slid into the seat next to him and handed him the mug of steaming coffee. "Excited?" he asked.

She nodded. "I haven't seen Jenny in months and Dante since the baby was born. I can't tell you how much your participation in the scheme to surprise me for Mother's Day means."

"Well, act a little surprised for Jenny's sake. She'd be disappointed to see how much Dante and his wife let the cat out of the bag."

"Dante knows I'm not crazy about surprises. Since Jenny loves surprises, she nurses the hope that I do too."

"Hmmmm. In the interest of avoiding surprises, I'd like to tell you that I invited all my kids in town over for dinner tonight to get to know you and your family. It'll probably be a madhouse."

She smiled. "It sounds wonderful. Give me the rundown on all of them again. There are so many, I get confused."

"David, his wife, two kids. Jared and his fiancée, Benita, and Donovan, my youngest boy. That's it here in St. Louis. The twins, Trent and Trey, are in New York."

"And Taylor's having job problems in Atlanta," Tiffany added.

"Add your son and daughter-in-law, grandchild, and daughter, Jenny—we have a houseful between us."

"What's for dinner? We're going to have to stop at the store," she said.

"No point in complicating things by cooking. I thought we'd order some authentic St. Louis thin crust pizza from Imo's, throw in a couple bottles of Chianti and call it a party."

Tiffany shifted uncomfortably at the mention of the Chianti wine. "Sounds good to me," she said. She looked out the car window at the blossoming trees as they headed north toward the airport to pick up her children.

Tiffany sat with Jason and her daughter Jenny in a restaurant near the airport eating breakfast and waiting for Dante's plane to come in. Jenny touched her mother's cheek. "You look great, Mom, you really do. Much more relaxed than I've seen you in a long while, maybe ever."

Tiffany smiled at her and wondered if sharing the secret

of the big "O" was an appropriate topic for mother-daughter conversation. She decided not. "Thanks, hon. I love it here in St Louis." She gazed at her daughter. "I love what you did to your hair," she said.

Jenny had highlighted her brown hair with gold tints that complemented her honeyed skin, and had a new relaxed pixyish cut that suited her perfectly. "But I have been worrying about something. You look like you've lost a little weight."

"Mom, I did that on purpose."

"Oh. You look a little thin."

Jenny shrugged. "At the rate I'm going, don't worry. I won't be too thin for long." She bit into a strawberry blintz loaded with cream cheese and swallowed it with satisfaction. "How's Kara and the baby?" she asked. "Is her pregnancy going well?"

"They are all doing great. Dante is growing like a weed and Kara's glowing with her pregnancy." Kara was Jenny's newly discovered half-sister and their relationship had had a rocky start to say the least, with a rivalry over a man. Kara had gotten the man, but Tiffany was happy to hear Jenny's concern, although she noted that Jenny carefully omitted Brent's name, her one-time fiancé and Kara's husband.

"I talked to Kara about a month ago. She was happy to hear about how well I was doing."

"So Mom, how are the meetings in the area? You've made a lot of big changes recently and I know how stressful that is to recovery."

Tiffany shifted in her seat and stole a glance at Jason. He was chewing on his pancakes, seemingly content to merely observe the reunion between mother and daughter rather than participate in the interchanges. But she knew he was as alert as ever to every word and nuance of what happened around him. She could almost visualize his ears tilting forward.

She picked at her cloth napkin in her lap, and as the

seconds ticked by, she realized her hesitation had been too long.

"So how is your recovery going?" Jenny asked.

"I haven't had time." Her words were thin and clipped.

Jenny looked puzzled, then aghast, then irritated. She shot a glance at Jason and sawed off another generous bit of blintz, obviously in lieu of whatever she wanted badly to say.

"Recovery from what?" Jason asked.

"It's nothing," Tiffany said as nonchalantly as she possibly could with a shrug and a wave of her hand. "Moving to St. Louis has been quite an adjustment. Socializing hasn't been high on my list of priorities," Tiffany added.

Jenny frowned and Tiffany felt her heart sink at Jason's quizzical look. He was going to ask her more and oh, God, what would she say? Why couldn't Jenny keep her mouth shut for once?

"We'd better hurry up. Dante's plane is due in twenty minutes," Jason murmured as he looked at his watch.

The house was full of people and laughter. Old school soul played in the background and the scent of pizza filled the air. Tiffany approached and embraced Jason from behind. He swung around and pulled her close for a little two-step. He let her go, laughed and refilled his glass of wine. He started to fill her glass also, but she remembered in time and covered it with a finger. She darted a glance at Jenny and yes, she was watching her with a slight frown. Tiffany turned away and filled her glass with diet Coke.

One of Jason's sons, Donovan, a handsome, animated young man, had thankfully approached Jenny and engaged her in conversation. Dante approached her and gently took the glass from her hand, took a sip and gave it back.

"You could have asked. I would have told you it's not alcoholic."

"I'm sorry, Mom. It's just I care about you so much and Jenny's got me worried. She says you've let your recovery slip."

"I'd say Jenny was overly concerned. She's been through extensive treatment herself and tends to project her own fears onto me. I have not slipped. I'm not going to slip. I've just moved to a new town and started a new job. I'm busy."

"I know." He hooked a hand around her waist and drew her close. "You've been through hell, Mom, and you've been so strong, supporting us and rebuilding your life from scratch. I think Jenny just wants the chance to worry about you for a change."

"I appreciate her concern, both of your concern, but now is not the time nor place to revive all the bad things that went on in the past." She couldn't keep her gaze from straying to Jason. He was deep in conversation with his son, Jared.

Dante's glance followed hers. "You like him a lot," Dante said.

Tiffany couldn't help the soft smile that lifted her lips. "A lot."

"He seems like a good man. A solid one with values, a million miles away from Sidney Eastman. I'm happy for you."

Tiffany's smile faltered as a dart of pain struck her that Dante couldn't yet say the word father, but always spoke of his father by name. "Jason is a wonderful man. But the relationship is new. I don't want any premature revelations. The past is better unfolded gradually."

Dante nodded, but looked concerned. "Jenny is right when she says that taking care of yourself is more important than anything. Old habits are easy to fall back on when—"

"Stop it, Dante," she said, her voice a low hiss. "I'm not a child, nor some incompetent fool. This is my life and it's not for my children to decide what I need to do or not.''

He looked down. "I'm sorry . . ."

She touched his arm, her heart filling with love for this man she'd carried within her, raised and nurtured. She loved both her children more than anything in the world. She'd felt a special sadness at the scars Dante had inside since he kept them so well hidden, unlike Jenny. She felt a similar special pride at the life and love Dante had managed to create for himself. He had turned out to be a wonderful man, an admirable man. He was able to give himself to a good woman fully and care for her with tender love and accept the same from her. So many men scarred by past pain weren't capable of that. Intimacy was the most fearful thing of all. She knew too well that it was the ones closest to you who could hurt you the most. "I love you, baby," she whispered to Dante.

He smiled at her with a crooked smile. "I know, Mom."

They both turned as they heard the sounds of welcome rippling through the room. A tall, slim man walked in with one of the most striking women she'd ever seen by his side and two young children bouncing with the energy of puppies. *It must be Jason's oldest son, David,* Tiffany thought. He looked the image of the picture of Diana that Jason had on the wall in a small room in the back of his house. His wife was the darkest person Tiffany had seen in a long time. Almost coal black with the bluish sheen of anthracite. Her skin was flawless and breathtakingly beautiful. Her features were soft and feminine and twisted locks hung down her back.

Something caught in her heart as she watched the happy reunion between Jason and his three healthy and handsome sons. They had a father who loved them and most importantly, set the example of what a man should be.

And look at them, strong and responsible with no shadow of past pain in their eyes like her Dante. Men like she'd never had in her life, strong men who were raised to provide and care for their family, both emotionally and physically. Wonderful men . . . like their father. She knew the arrow that pierced her heart was love, and she wanted to gasp at the pain of it and cry because she'd been afraid she'd never in her life be able to feel the sweetness of love past her first bloom of youth. Love all the more painful when mixed with uncertainty. Would Jason ever love her? She bit her lip, thinking of her former husband Sidney Eastman and how much he'd hurt her. What if she wasn't good enough to be . . . She banished the thought and lifted her chin.

Tiffany Eastman was a survivor, she affirmed to herself. She was a good woman and worthy of any man's love. Look at her children. She brought them through the fire and they were all right. Especially Dante. Other than the hurt around his eyes, he was unscathed by the storms of his childhood. That mattered more than anything.

Chapter 10

"Jared, do you have something to say to me?" Benita asked.

He took a large bite of Imo's pizza to stall, chewed, swallowed and washed it down with Chianti.

"Jared?"

"Why do you ask right now? I thought we could talk later."

"Your father asked if you'd talked to me. He shook his head when I said no, but wouldn't tell me what was going on. What do you need to talk to me about?"

He reached for another piece of pizza, but Benita's voice froze him.

"I want to know what's up. Now." Her voice was soft, but he could hear the undercurrent of strain.

He shrugged. "I was having second thoughts."

"Second thoughts about what, Jared?" Her voice softened to a whisper and he had to lean forward to hear her.

"The marriage and all."

Silence.

"We shouldn't talk about it now, really. There's a party going on." He dared a glance at her face. It looked like white marble.

"We are getting married," she said.

He picked up a piece of pizza.

"We are getting married, aren't we?" she asked.

He wished that a hole in the floor would open up and swallow him up. Bad thing was that he wondered if Benita were wishing the same thing.

"Let me tell you something," she continued. "I got a call at home from some woman last night."

Oh hell, he thought.

"She had an interesting tale to tell. It appears that your old girlfriend is running around babbling about how you dumped 'that witch' and now you're going to marry her."

He swallowed hard.

"Don't touch that goddamn pizza," she said, her voice rising, and his hand snapped back. He hadn't realized he'd reached for it.

Benita, a gently reared, upper middle-class white woman from the Atlanta suburbs, stood and put a hand on her hip. Then she did the neck roll thing. He couldn't believe his eyes. The woman had transformed into a sistah. A mad sistah.

"I'm waiting for you to say something. I'm hoping you say something that makes a drop of sense or I'm gonna . . ." She let the words trail away, but he had no doubt she meant to say she was gonna kick his black ass.

He looked around at his father and brothers in mute appeal. Dad was leaning against the wall, an eyebrow raised and a clear look of I-told-you-so on his face. David looked interested, Donovan looked like he was going to crack up and fall on the floor laughing, the son of a bitch. He knew better than to look at the women.

"Not now, Benita. It's really not appropriate. Let's go and talk about this somewhere private."

"Was it appropriate for you to go and try to sleep with someone else two weeks before our wedding?" she yelled. "Was it private to tell every goddamn person you came across that you regretted asking me to marry you?"

Apparently he'd said the wrong thing. You could hear a pin drop in the room as all listened for his answer.

He reached for her arm so he could draw her away. "We need to talk."

She flinched away from him. "I gave you your chance for talking and you didn't take it, you sorry son of a . . . Never mind. We are done. Just let me get out of here. You are not worth the drama." She cast about for her purse, grabbed it and was out the door.

"If you have any hope of salvaging the relationship, I suggest you follow her," his father drawled.

Jared heard a car door slamming, the engine revving and tires burning. Damn. She had the keys to his car and in her mood the woman might push it into the river for fun.

"You can take my car," his dad said, holding out his keys.

"Thanks." Jared grabbed the keys and shot an evil glance at his brother Donovan, who was whispering in Jenny's ear, laughing.

Jared pulled up at Benita's place and parked behind his car. It was parked up on the curb. He really didn't feel like confronting Benita and dealing with this right now. Every male instinct in his body was telling him to book and get out of Tombstone before high noon. He got out of the car with every muscle in his stomach clenched. The echo of his father's voice telling him to be a man rang in his ears. He hadn't been much of one, ducking and dodging instead of facing what he dreaded most—the woman he was supposed to marry.

He rang the doorbell. Benita threw the door open. "Well?" she said.

He rubbed the back of his neck. "Before you start cussing or looking for knives, I want to tell you that I'm sorry. I've been an ass. We need to talk."

"How could you? How could you embarrass me like this?" She walked into the house and sank down on the sofa. He followed, with more than a little trepidation.

"Panic? Stupidity? Y chromosomes?" Jared said. He pulled a chair from the dinette set in the corner and sat down.

"Well, as long as you've recovered." She took out a tissue from her purse and blew her nose. "I had to change the menu for the reception appetizers. The caterer is incompetent and it's too late to change." She looked at him. "I don't expect to ever be embarrassed by public infidelity again when we're married."

"Hold up, Benita. I said I'd been a jackass for not talking to you sooner, but we are not getting married."

"What did you say?"

Her voice ended on a disbelieving shriek and Jared swallowed. Maybe he wasn't being very tactful with his approach, but he'd jumped from the board and there was nothing left to do but hit the water. "I don't think marriage is the right thing for us right now—"

"So that woman was right. You're going back to that mealy mouthed stupid witch you dated before me?"

Oh, God, he thought. *Here it comes.*

"You can't do this to me. How dare you humiliate me like this? Who the hell do you think you are?"

"I know who I am. I just don't want us both to make the biggest mistake—"

He saw something hurling toward him out of the corner of his eye and he ducked just in time to see a glass vase crash on the wall a few inches from his head. Damn, the girl had a mean right arm. "There is no reason to—"

Was that a lamp she was hurling? Damn. He ducked again. The lamp fell short as it yanked the cord from the wall.

"You're a psychotic, woman-hating bastard!" Benita screamed. "You lied and told me you loved me, dragged me almost to the altar, then dumped me in front of my friends and family. Am I just some fool, some stupid white girl that you could brag on to your homeboys that you *played?* Is that it, you black bastard?"

He fell back and eyed the door. A quick sprint and he could be out of Dodge.

She preempted him and darted in front of his escape route with her neck swiveling. "No, we are going to finish this. N****r, you ain't going no damn where."

What did she say to him? Now, while it was a black chick's privilege to call him the n-word in the heat of a fight, Benita was white and she'd just gone too far. Rage shot through him like a flash flood. "And why are you so eager to marry a black man? Is it just to hurt your father? Is it?" The words slipped out before he could recall them.

"How dare you bring my father into this."

Jared raised an eyebrow. "Your mother and I had a talk. She said ever since they had the surprise of your little sister born into the family when you were eighteen, you've been insanely jealous of your father's attention. I saw myself how you were with him. You were up under him every time he even glanced in your little sister's direction. And now—now you've gotten daddy's attention in a big way, haven't you?"

She slapped his face, hard. Jared's eyes narrowed, but he didn't move.

"I loved you. How could you do this to me?" Tears welled in her eyes and she suddenly looked like a lost child. "Please tell me that this is not happening. Just tell me that."

Suddenly he wanted to wave his hand and make everything all right for her, but he couldn't. He couldn't marry her. He simply couldn't.

"I'm sorry," he said.

Her face transformed from innocence and pain to ugliness and anger in a second's time. "You are going to pay," she said, her voice low and shaking with anger. "You are going to pay for my embarrassment and every penny my family has spent on this wedding."

"I'll pay gladly," he said. "You wouldn't want to marry someone like me anyway. Your family and friends will be very understanding."

The words sat there for a few seconds. Then Benita squared her shoulders and lifted her chin. "You're right," she said. "They will." She stepped away from the door.

On Sunday morning, Mother's Day, Tiffany heard a soft tap at her door. She rolled over in bed and plumped the pillows behind her, sitting up. Jason and she had decorously slept apart in anticipation of this moment.

"Come in," she called.

Dante and Jenny walked in as she expected with a steaming tray and a vase with a yellow rosebud in it. A wide smile broke out on her face at the sight. It was a Mother's Day tradition of years standing, the breakfast in bed her children had prepared. It had been too many years since they'd been together to enjoy this. Dante settled the tray across her knees and they both sat on each side of her.

She solemnly took a bite of the pancake topped with strawberries and cream, her favorite. "How is it?" Jenny asked.

"Like sugar and spice with a touch of snail and puppy dog tail," was the ritual answer. They all laughed in delight and Tiffany was transported to twenty years ago with her young children at her side laughing joyously. They were the best things she'd done in her life. They were what she'd lived for and the only reason she'd chosen to keep on going through the emotional pain that almost did her in. She loved her children so much she could taste it, like a good hurting inside.

They'd come a long way together. "Come here," she said, and she pulled them both to her, hugging them fiercely. "There's nowhere but up for us to go. I want you two to stop worrying about me. I'm strong and whole and so are you. We've all been through hell, but we've healed. We have long, happy lives in front of us and I want us to keep savoring the present and looking forward. We have to leave the past dead and buried where it belongs."

"Amen," Dante said.

Jenny buried her face in Tiffany's neck. "Mom, I love you so much. Happy Mother's Day."

When she lifted her head, Tiffany pinched her nose gently like she had when Jenny was six. "Let's eat."

They each picked up a fork and dug in together like they'd done many Mother's Days before and would for many more to come.

"So what are your plans for summer?" Tiffany asked her daughter. They sat on the porch swing together, sipping herb tea and enjoying the morning air.

"I've been meaning to bring that up with you. I don't really want to spend the summer in DC. I'd like to do some traveling, but I don't have the funds for that."

"Maybe we should spend some time together," Tiffany said. "It's been a long time since it's been just you and I."

"Yes. We haven't been together since my father died."

Tiffany reached out and touched Jenny's hand. "That's over now, and I'm proud of you. The past is dead and buried."

"That would be nice in a sense, but I believe that the

past never dies, it just becomes a part of us. That's why it can rear its ugly head up and bite us in the butt if we ignore it."

A tinge of irritation touched Tiffany. "What are you getting at, Jenny?"

"If I come and spend the summer with you, it wouldn't just be you and I. You've started a new relationship with a man."

"Is that your point? You resent my happiness now so you are continually bringing up the problems that happened in the past?"

"That's not fair, Mom. I haven't mentioned a word about your recovery or the past since you tripped when I first arrived. But how wonderful can this relationship be if you are so afraid that this man won't accept who you are?"

Tiffany put down her teacup on the little weathered wicker table. Her irritation was tempered by the knowledge that Jenny was right, and she was talking out of concern and love.

"He accepts me. I simply see no point in bringing up a lot of unpleasantness which, I repeat, as far as I'm concerned, was dead and buried with Sidney."

Jenny sighed and sipped her tea. "This isn't easy for me to bring up to you. But to be honest, I'm sick with worry. I was serious when I mentioned the past biting you on the butt. You are too anxious about it. Also, with all the changes and stress you're facing, is it a wise time to neglect your recovery?"

"Don't think I don't appreciate your concern about me. And I do realize it is out of care. But let me handle this area of my life, hon. I don't feel all that comfortable discussing it with my child."

"Okay." Jenny stared into the distance for a moment. "Would it bother you if I spent the summer in St. Louis?" she asked.

"No. I'd love it. But where would you stay?"

"I was talking to Jason about my classes and he asked if I was staying in Maryland for the summer. When I mentioned I was at loose ends, he invited me to stay here. He said something about missing kids in the house. I didn't really consider it at the time, but the more I think about it, maybe it wouldn't be a bad idea."

"It's a great idea. I'd love to have you here and I feel Jason's recently empty nest has rocked him more than he admits."

"I agree. Those sons of his sure are fine."

"Like father, like sons. I saw that you and Donovan hit it off well."

Jenny grinned. "Yes, we did. But did you get an eyeful of that Jared. Shoot, he looks good."

"Unfortunately he's taken."

"From the sound of that fight he and that woman had, it doesn't seem like that's going to be the case for long."

"Perhaps not," Tiffany said. She narrowed her eyes at her daughter, but held her tongue. Lord knows Jenny didn't have the best track record with men.

"Don't worry, Mom, I'm cool," Jenny said. "I just liked the looks of him, that's all."

Chapter 11

"Little Dante is going to miss Grandma," Celeste said.

"Not nearly as much as I'm going to miss him," Tiffany cooed at her grandchild. "He's a fine baby. Very secure and loved."

Celeste beamed at the compliment. "Thanks. Sometimes I have to pinch myself to make sure it's real. I've got it all. A man I'm crazy in love with, a perfect little baby, the opportunity to work at home, everything. Sometimes I think the gods would be jealous."

"You deserve every bit of it. You've worked hard and you've made my son very happy. So your graphic art business is doing well?"

"Booming. I've had to contract out work."

"I'm glad to hear it."

Tiffany headed up the highway in silence for a while. They'd taken both their cars to take Jenny and Dante and his family back to the airport to avoid the squeeze they'd experienced before.

"Jenny and Donovan really hit it off."

Tiffany's brow creased as she remembered what Jenny had said about Jared. Her daughter had a track record of getting with the wrong man and overlooking the right ones. "I hope so," she murmured.

"If they want to keep in touch, they will. When I first met Dante, remember he lived in DC and I was in Charlotte."

"It would be good for Jenny. Donovan is a nice young man."

Celeste glanced at her out of the corner of her eye. "So is his father."

"If you only knew how nice," Tiffany answered.

Celeste giggled. "I bet I could guess."

"Maybe you could," Tiffany answered with a grin. The visit with the kids had been wonderful, but she couldn't deny she was looking forward to having Jason all to herself again alone in the big house. His brand of loving was addictive.

Tiffany pulled in the garage after she dropped the kids off. She'd stopped at a novelty shop on the way back from the airport and picked up an assortment of such delicacies as flavored oils and honey-flavored body powder. She'd hesitated over the edible panties, but thought that would be too much. She couldn't wait to feel his touch, his warm and loving lips on her body. She scarcely realized what had come over her. With this man she felt like a wanton woman, a nymphomaniac at her age. She'd always been relieved when sex wasn't expected before and now she was ready to beg for it. She dreamed about it when she wasn't with him, craved it more when she was. For the first time in her life she . . . touched herself. What was happening to her? *In heat, baby, the man's got you in heat. Don't let him get away, you may never recapture this feeling again.*

She walked in and sat her bag of goodies on the table when he approached. She turned toward him, affection and desire in her eyes, and expected him to take her in his arms.

He took a little step back. "We need to talk."

"Okay." Disappointed and a touch apprehensive, she trailed him to his office. He sat behind his desk like he was about to interview her for a job.

He clasped his hands in front of him. "Am I correct in assuming that you have a problem with alcohol?"

She couldn't breathe for a moment. "No, you are not correct in assuming anything about a problem of mine. Is there anything else you want to ask me?"

"I got the impression that your daughter said you were an alcoholic. Is it true?"

A storm of anger caught her up so suddenly she almost gasped. "What if it were?"

"You should have told me you are an alcoholic before you moved into my home."

"I had no idea your offer had so many strings."

"Tiffany." His voice was tense with strain. "I'm a cardio-vascular surgeon. I've seen some of my colleagues struggle with alcohol. I simply think it would be better if we faced something of this magnitude together."

Emotion rushed through her. Was it fear? Or was it anger? "How do you have any idea of what I have to face? You know nothing about me. Nothing," she said.

"I admit that we haven't taken the time to learn the intimate details of each other's lives. This thing has rushed over us like a wildfire. But your alcoholism scares me. It's so different from anything I've known. I don't think I could tolerate your drinking."

She blinked, but a second was not long enough to stop her fear from exploding into anger and overcoming reason. "I'll tell you what, you don't have to tolerate a damned thing more from me. I'm out of here." She whirled and strode out of the room toward her bedroom.

She got her suitcase from the closet and started ripping

clothes from the hangers. Her chest burned. He was rejecting her. All right. So be it. She was getting the hell out. She swept her underwear from a drawer with one hand and dumped it onto the suitcase. She did what she had to do yet again—flee from a man. Except somehow it was worse because at this moment she didn't know if she'd survive this rejection.

"Tiffany."

"Get out of here. Haven't you said enough? I'm leaving. Just—" She swallowed a sob. No way was she going to cry. "Just get out of here and let me pack."

"I can't let you go, baby."

"You don't have a choice. I'm not going to let you hurt me."

Jason stepped back, his face still. "I told you how I felt. This is something we need to deal with and here you are ready to run out on me. What is this all about?"

"You condemned me without a fair trial."

"I did not. I told you how I felt about alcoholism and expressed my disappointment that you haven't leveled with me."

"Level with you about what? I haven't touched alcohol for three years."

"Three years?"

"Damn straight. Then there you go ranting about what you will or won't tolerate. You can stick—"

"Tiffany. Stop it. What are you so scared of? I don't want to hurt you."

Her breath caught in her throat. He'd spoken her fear out loud. She was running because she was afraid he would hurt her. And he could so easily. Jason Cates held her heart in the palm of his hand.

"Let's talk," he said. "Come into the den. I'll make coffee."

A few minutes later, Tiffany curled up on the opposite end of the couch, as far as she could get away from him.

She watched the steam rise from the coffee, climb into the air and dissipate.

"I've seen the world in black and white for so long," Jason said. "This is right, this is wrong—no shades of gray. Intellectually knowing the shade exists is one thing. Emotionally knowing is another. Do you understand what I mean?"

She nodded at his words and wished her old ghosts from the past would disappear just like that steam. She fantasized that she was one of those fictional women who washed up on far shores with amnesia. Their pasts were erased and all was forgotten. A clean slate and a new beginning. Lucky women.

"I'm a churchgoing man," he continued. "But I always was lax compared to Diana. She was a God-fearing woman."

She stiffened at the mention of his late wife's name.

"She didn't believe in smoking and drinking spirits at all. I'm telling all this so you will understand that this is not an easy adjustment for me to make," Jason said.

He paused, but she lay quiet, waiting. "I've not only allowed a woman into Diana's home for the first time in thirty years, into her bedroom, and now I discover that you're an alcoholic. It scares me."

"It shouldn't," she whispered.

"Why? What am I going to have to deal with? Drunken rages and sloppiness? Alcoholic stupors?"

She flinched away from him and straightened, turning her face away from him. "I don't deserve that."

"Maybe you don't. I'm speaking frankly of my fears."

"I'm not drinking now. It's an unpleasant fact of my past, true, but I've moved on."

"I guess we can put the past behind us."

Tiffany lifted her head and stared at him. "Can we? Can we really? I'm not your Diana. I will never be your Diana. My name is Tiffany Eastman and I drank to soothe my misery for years. I kept it together quite well for a legislative wife. I certainly wasn't the only one in my condition. I was not given to drunken rages but rather morose silences. I only drank when the sun went down. I stopped drinking when I left my husband and checked myself into a drug and alcohol rehabilitation center."

Jason started to open his mouth to say something, but she raised her hand. "Wait, there's more. My daughter Jenny followed in my footsteps. She's a convicted felon for drunken driving and manslaughter. She spent over a year in a security treatment center. My late husband shot my son, beat me, then tried to kill me, and ended up killing himself. So I suppose you could say madness runs in the family also. I suppose that's enough for now. Do you still think we can work this out?"

Jason opened his mouth and closed it. "I don't want to let you go," he said. "The thought of you not being here with me makes me feel . . . We can work it out." He drew her away from the couch and into his arms.

He lowered his head and his lips touched hers softly. He pulled her to him and she couldn't resist the strong authority of his arms. He fit her body next to his and deepened the kiss to telegraph his passionate need. He turned away with a groan and took her hand to lead her to the bedroom. She followed. Sexual healing, Tiffany thought. She'd allow his body to take away her foreboding fears. Sometimes too much talking opened too many wounds.

A little while afterward, she traced the line of his cheek. "How are we going to work it out, Jason?" she asked again.

His eyes fluttered open and met hers, then looked away. "You say you haven't touched alcohol in almost three years. What is there to work out? The past is dead."

She thought of Diana. But not forgotten. "Do you accept me?" Tiffany asked. "Sometimes I feel as if you believe I don't . . . measure up."

"Of course I accept you. I misunderstood, Tiffany. I

thought you were an active alcoholic and I knew I couldn't deal with that."

"How do you feel about who I was?"

"I feel that you're a remarkable woman."

"So why were you so quick to label me and believe the worst?"

Jason rubbed his eyes. "Let's drop it, Tiffany."

She was silent, but anxiety and doubts swirled within her. Something wasn't right. They were glossing over something they needed to thrash out sooner rather than later, but she needed him with every fiber of her body. She couldn't push it. He didn't understand.

That was fine because it was no longer a problem. She hadn't touched a drop of alcohol since she'd walked out of Sidney's house into that treatment center. She was just fine, a normal person. Normal people don't go around giving themselves negative labels and meeting to obsess over past habits that are no longer part of their lives.

"Consider it dropped," she said with a light kiss on his lips.

"She called me the N word, Dad," Jared said.

Jason raised an eyebrow. He'd heard more about his son's troubles with women in the past few weeks than he'd heard in the past few years. It was confusing, but fascinating. When he was a young man the only woman he'd dealt with was Diana. The number of women and the accompanying drama that some of his sons went through was amazing. "It could have simply been the extreme stress of the moment and the need to lash out at you. I wouldn't put too much on it." Jason shook his head. "You dated her long enough that you should know her character."

Jared shrugged. "What does that have to do with hidden racism?"

"What if a black woman called you the same thing? The

way you were acting she probably would have called you that and a few other choice names too."

"That's different."

"Is it? In my eyes you come off as bad or worse than she does, racist or no. She should have gone upside your head."

"She tried, but her aim was off." He moved his jaw gingerly. "Though she did slap me one. That woman has a mean right." Jared got up to throw his second empty beer can into the trash, and he went to the refrigerator to get another one.

"So, have you bought the diamond for Stacie yet?"

Jared shifted uncomfortably. "I was going to wait and see if Benita gives me her rock back first," he mumbled.

Jason tried to suppress his chuckle and succeeded. "I wouldn't count on it. I heard the plan was for her to pawn it and pay her parents back for their trouble, deposits and what not. So again, when are you going to get Stacie's rock?"

Jared fell back on the couch and closed his eyes. "Maybe I should run off to Tibet and join a monastery or something. Offer my medical services."

"You don't want to marry her either? Not ready to commit? Not ready to settle down?"

"I don't think so. I like dating her. Hell, I like dating Benita too if it comes down to that. I don't want to marry either of them. It seems that women want me so much and lately—"

Jason couldn't keep a hoot of laughter from escaping. "Oh my God! My son has transformed into some limp wrist who has no idea what he wants from a woman." Jason flopped his wrist around. "It is still women, huh?"

"You're enjoying this, Dad, aren't you? Admit it. You always said I was going to get mine."

"It is sort of entertaining. You've dogged too many women over the years, son. Your ways are catching up with you. Since you were eight years old you had a swarm of little girls buzzing around. I always had this vision of women storming my front porch with pitchforks and torches clamoring for a piece of your butt."

"I get it honest. Remember that nurse who holed up in here naked to surprise you?"

"And surprised three of my sons instead? How could I forget?" Jason chuckled at the memory.

"That was the high point of my junior high years. But the point is that women have always swarmed over you too and you haven't settled down with one either. Until now, anyway," Jared said.

Jason felt uneasy. "You're talking about Tiffany."

"Yeah. We are blown away that you finally moved a woman into Mom's house. When are the wedding bells?"

"I believe we were discussing your mess," Jason answered.

"Dad, I got to admit you got it right about a mess. I still can't believe that I told Stacie that I'd give her a ring."

"Your timing was off to say the least. I can't believe that such a competent surgeon could be so downright stupid with women. I can't wait to see how you get out of this one."

"Thank you for your sympathy and encouragement, Dad."

"You're quite welcome." Jason popped the top off another beer and chuckled at the look on his son's face. The boy needed a spanking and it looked like his women were going to be the ones who gave it to him.

Chapter 12

Jason sipped his coffee as he pretended to read the newspaper, the words blurring in front of his eyes. He was weak-willed. He turned a page and almost ripped it with the force of emotion that played through him. No self-discipline. No, that wasn't correct, he had no self-discipline when it concerned Tiffany. She had only to smile at him and he melted. She only had to touch him with a fingertip and he couldn't dream of not making love to her.

Here he was talking about his son Jared, and he'd lost his own mind over a woman. It was uncomfortable to say the least. He hadn't had this out-of-control feeling since he'd first met Diana at fourteen. Did he want his orderly, routine life back the way it was before Tiffany appeared— when his emotions were an unrippled, still, deep pond? But the thought of Tiffany ever leaving him made him feel sick. She churned him into a stormy sea. She took his breath away, made him feel delirious and he didn't know whether it was panic or joy. Love?

That thought made him pick up the paper again and

try to fill his mind with the unrest in the eastern European countries and the latest baseball stats. He heard her car driving into the garage. He carefully laid the paper down and went to help her carry the groceries in.

"You like salmon?" she asked. "There was some on sale and I got a lot. I hope you like it. I love grilled salmon."

"I like salmon," he said. He smelled her perfume as she passed, a complicated scent grounded with earthy, woody tones and topped with the hint of fruit and mimosa. It reminded him of her more personal scent, sweet and musky. The memory almost made him groan. He wanted her, wanted her constantly, wanted her continuously.

She was bending over, stacking some cans into a lower cupboard. The curve of her bottom beckoned him, and his knowledge of the enticing secrets underneath excited him. He was suffering some version of male menopause that turned conservative, thoughtful men into randy old goats.

He reached out; his fingers knew the soft warmth of her. Desire rocked him. She drew in a breath and faced him.

They feverishly tore at each other's clothes and the next thing he realized he had her pinned up against the refrigerator. He raised her smooth brown thigh to his waist and entered her wet warmth with one stroke. Quick, hot and frantic, they pounded down the road to completion. Sweet, too sweet. With something like a sob, he thrust deep within her when he felt the pulsing throbs of her climax around him, and his own ecstatic spasms racked him.

Afterward they collapsed on the floor amid the groceries, and he held her close. He dropped a kiss on the top of her head and glanced at his watch. From zero to blastoff within the space of ten minutes. That had to be a record. "Have we regressed to adolescence?" he mused.

"Sometimes I think so. But that's a good thing, isn't it? Think of all these men having to run out and get Viagra," she said with a grin. "I'm going to take a quick shower and I'll let you finish putting up the groceries, all right?"

When she returned he'd showered, changed and put up the rest of the groceries. She smiled at him and reached in the refrigerator for the salmon. "I'll put this on to marinate if you'll fire up the grill."

"Sounds good to me. But remember I'm on call this weekend." He pointed at the beeper on his belt. "He's the master and I'm the slave."

Like it knew it was being talked about the beeper went off and Jason sighed as he reached for the phone. When he got off, Tiffany was staring into the refrigerator. She was reaching for the beer when she suddenly froze and took out a diet Coke instead. He watched her and felt chilled. She still wanted alcohol. He'd get rid of every drop of alcohol in the house as soon as he could.

"Tiffany?"

"Uh-huh?"

"Got any plans for next weekend?"

"I'm yours." She entered the room and stretched out on the couch next to him and popped open her can. "Is this the Braves game?"

"Yes."

"Good," she said and settled in.

He loved a woman who liked sports, he'd discovered. He knew there were a lot out there, but this was the first one he'd met. He studied Tiffany's profile. She was intelligent, cultured, a wonderful conversationalist, and she oozed class from her very fingertips. But she was an ex-alcoholic, an abused spouse; her past had been ugly and sordid by any standards. She'd been through a lot. He felt a surge of protectiveness mixed with guilt. Why was he worried about her alcoholism so much? She'd been abstinent for three years. It was a dark shadow that touched the edge of his growing desire for her.

"I almost forgot to mention this," he said. "An old

friend of mine is getting married in Atlanta and I planned to attend.''

"Great. I like St. Louis, but I still miss Atlanta. And it will be great to see Taylor too." Tiffany turned her attention to the game on TV as the sound of the crack of a bat was followed by the crowd's roar. "Home run," she murmured. "Damn."

"I'm planning to go to church tomorrow," he announced.

She looked at him. "I hadn't gotten as far as looking at possible churches I could attend in St. Louis."

"I used to rarely miss a Sunday before you came. I wish you would come with me."

She curled her fingers around his. "It will be wonderful to go to church with you."

"Good." He sighed with contentment, laid his head in her lap and gazed at the television, the shadow of worry forgotten.

When Jason walked into Pilgrim Rest Baptist Church with Tiffany on his arm, he felt a flush of pride. She stood out like a diamond among cubic zirconium. She wore a simple dark gold sheath that revealed her every womanly curve without losing an iota of her modesty. The color made her warm chocolate skin glow. She was beautiful. He intercepted some jealous and downright evil glances from other women, a few of whom he'd dated, and moved closer to her. *Get over it,* he thought. *There's no way you can compare with her.*

He introduced her around and she handled herself like a queen, gracious, friendly, remembering names with an aptitude he could only admire. A politician's wife.

"Brother Cates, Brother Cates." He turned and with some trepidation saw Twila Hensley bearing down on him. She was the choir director and she'd asked him out on a date once. He'd reluctantly accepted. Christian charity, he supposed, mixed with a little sheer fear. The woman outweighed him by nearly a hundred pounds and stood eye to eye with him. He wasn't a short man. Twila obviously had no intention of brooking deferments, excuses or any other form of weaseling out of the date, so he squared his shoulders and got it over with. To say the date had been an ordeal was an understatement. She had taken him dancing. Her dance specialty was "The Bump." 'Nuff said.

At the end of the evening Twila Hensley had tried to kiss him good night and tell him when their next date would be. It was cowardice that made him profess that his undying love for his dead wife had condemned him to miserable bachelorhood, and any more dates with her would be too much of a temptation. Then he'd limped his bruised and battered body into his house to soak in Epsom salts and put the awful experience behind him.

"How can I help you, Sister Hensley?" he asked.

She smiled at him. "And who might this be?" she moved toward Tiffany, her smile stretching and becoming as fake as the gaudy matching necklace and earrings she wore.

"This is my houseguest, Tiffany Eastman. Tiffany, this is the choir director, Sister Twila Hensley."

"It's a pleasure to meet you," Tiffany said with a smile. Twila cast a glance up and down Tiffany's form and said, "Oh, so that's your houseguest. I've heard quite a bit about her." She turned her back to her and faced Jason. "We had quite a musical program planned, but one of our soloists is ill and there is nobody to replace her. It's a very well-known tune." She swung around back to Tiffany. "Honey, you do sing, don't you? Can you fill in?"

Alarm shot through Jason. He knew it didn't work like that. Strangers didn't get suddenly invited to do solos at the drop of a hat. Twila was setting Tiffany up for a fall. What was it with women sometimes that they had to be so evil, Jason thought, exasperated, as he opened his mouth to set Sister Hensley straight.

"I'd be delighted," Tiffany was saying.

Jason blinked rapidly. "Honey . . ." he started to say.

"Honey?" Twila said in a shrill voice. People's heads swiveled. "When are the wedding bells?" she demanded.

He was speechless.

"What is the selection you'd like me to sing, Sister Hensley?" Tiffany asked, apparently unruffled.

"His Eye Is on the Sparrow."

Jason's stomach sank. A difficult song and one that the singer would have to sing very well to pull off as a solo. He glanced down at Tiffany. He didn't think she was a churchgoing woman. She might not have any idea of what she was getting into.

"I love that song," she was saying.

"Good. We'll put you up there first. C'mon chile, let's go find you a robe. Do you know what a cappella means?" Twila asked as she hustled Tiffany away.

Lord have mercy, Jason thought, with all the fervency of a heartfelt prayer.

Jason willed himself not to bite his fingernails, a bad habit he'd overcome more than thirty-five years ago, as the choir stood and Tiffany walked to the front and approached the mike. She wore a gold and ruby robe and held herself with an aura of confidence and authenticity. She was quality, she was real and she knew it.

The opening chords of the song started and the rest of the choir stood. Jason took a second thinking of imaginative tortures for the fiend Twila Hensley before he closed his eyes and braced himself for Tiffany's possible embarrassment.

A hush palpably swept through the church as the music

ceased and the choir silenced. Then a voice rose, high, sweet and full, like a sparrow.

Why should I feel discouraged,
Why should the shadows come . . .

Jason's eyes opened and his jaw dropped. Richness, spirit and soul issued from Tiffany's throat. Her head was thrown back and her eyes closed and the melody was a part of her.

His eye is on the sparrow . . .

Even a cappella and a step back from the microphone, her voice easily filled the place to bursting. It swooped and dived and carried the spirit on its wings.

I sing because I'm happy,
I sing because I'm free . . .

Jason saw the hands going up in the air, the people nodding. "Yes, Lord Jesus . . . sing it, girl . . . that's right."

He couldn't stop the grin that spread over his face. Black folks let you know readily of their enjoyment or displeasure. Tiffany had them in the palms of her delicate hands.

For His eye is on the sparrow,
And I know He watches me.

Twila Hensley motioned toward the choir and its collective voice rose, but Tiffany's words still soared above them.

Let not your heart be troubled,
His tender word I hear . . .

The shouts from the churchgoers added to the old melody. Jason felt his guilt fade away and an inner peace fill him. Everything had to be all right. It was going to be fine. Tiffany had laid her gift before the Lord and it had been accepted with love, spirit and joy.

And resting on His goodness,
I lose my doubts and fears . . .

Chapter 13

Tiffany twined her fingers through Jason's and leaned against his shoulder as she felt the airplane's acceleration push her back in the seat. No matter how many times she flew, she couldn't get over her nervousness at takeoffs and landings. She took a deep breath. She wasn't as excited about this Atlanta trip as she thought she would be. The timing could be better. The stress and strain of starting a new job still pulled her through the week, and the stress of a new relationship with Jason pulled her through the weekend. Not that he wasn't wonderful. But starting a new relationship, no matter how good, could be a strain. When a person gains something precious, what comes with it is a new fear. Fear of loss. She'd read somewhere that many new lottery winners' overall life happiness drastically decreased after the first year because of mismanagement, greedy friends and relatives and above all the fear of losing what they felt they'd never really earned.

Jason was her lottery. The intelligent, accomplished, handsome, gentle, loving man she'd always dreamed of having. At forty-seven she'd hit the jackpot. So why was she so afraid she was going to blow it or someone or something was going to take this happiness from her? It was a stupid foreboding and she wasn't stupid.

"I ordered the wedding gift from their register. The store will deliver it to our hotel in Atlanta all wrapped so we don't have to worry about that," Jason said.

"So how long has it been since you've seen your friend?" she asked.

"I saw Marvin at a conference last year. Don't let him intimidate you. He's very outspoken. And from what I hear his fiancée isn't much better. They're good people though."

"Were they together for a long time?" Curiosity filled her about how a couple at their age met and fell in love.

"Not long. Her daughter was his private duty nurse and recently married his son. Marvin had some medical problems crop up a while back, but I gather he's better now."

"How romantic."

"I gather you're talking about Marvin's son's marriage and not his medical problems?"

She grinned at him. "No, I don't find your friend's medical problems in the least romantic. In fact, speaking of medical problems, there is a certain male gland that frequently causes problems in men around your age. I have nightmares about . . . how shall I delicately put it? The effect of treatment of such on potency."

Now he grinned and poked her gently in the ribs, "Quit it. The only thing keeping you up at night is the reality of my potency."

"Hmmmmmm. I always wondered why this is such a touchy subject with men. Maybe it's because like their psyches, the very fragility . . ."

Jason leaned over and kissed her.

"Have you heard of the mile high club?" Tiffany asked.

"I know the lavatory might be a little cramped, but I always wanted to be initiated."

His eyes widened.

"You could go first and I'd join you. We'd have a secret knock. Three taps, a pause, another knock . . ."

"I can't believe you're tempting me to go do it in an airplane bathroom," Jason murmured. He leaned over to her and his tongue brushed against her ear, followed by a trail of nibbling kisses down her neck. It felt good.

"When the seat-belt light goes off, we can—"

She giggled, sighed and moved away from him. "We'd better not. I just remembered that somebody told me that mature adults with adult children don't fornicate in tiny, uncomfortable airplane lavatories."

"I wonder who made up that rule?" he said, his fingers starting to wander in an intimate direction.

Tiffany glanced across the aisle at the people reading newspapers. "Down, boy. Be good."

"Tease," Jason said with a grin. He pulled a magazine out of the pocket in front of him. "This is going to be a long, boring flight."

"It's barely an hour." Tiffany smiled to herself. She couldn't resist teasing him and turning him on. She was crazy about the man. She had no idea how she would ever do without him. The last glimmer of her earlier fears blew away and faded into the distance.

The ring of the phone broke her slumber. Tiffany peeked over Jason's unmoving shoulder at the alarm clock. It was almost nine. Goodness. She nudged him a little and he reached out, eyes still closed, and grabbed the phone.

"Taylor," he mumbled, and she grabbed the phone from him.

"Taylor! I missed you," she cried into the phone. Jason

covered his head with a pillow and burrowed into the blankets.

"You won't believe what's happened. I've got a new job," Taylor said.

"What? You loved working at that battered woman's agency."

"The agency closed."

"Why? That's unbelievable. What happened?"

"Long story. I'll tell you later, but get this. I'm working in my fiancé's detective agency."

Tiffany sat up in the bed.

"Fiancé? Detective? What's going on? Are you telling me you're getting *married*?" The last word came out a shriek and Jason groaned from within his nest of covers.

"Yes! I'm getting married."

"I don't believe it." Tiffany shook Jason, beside herself with excitement. "Your daughter's getting married."

He raised his head and squinted at her. "Who's the fool?" he asked, with only the shadow of a grin. Tiffany thumped his head with a pillow.

"Did you hear your father? He wants to know who the fool is."

"The extremely lucky man is Stone Emerson. Remember him?"

"Of course. So you finally gave in to the feeling. I was wondering if you would. You fought it so hard."

"Sometimes a girl makes a mistake or two. But I have more than made up for it. Guess what the name of our detective agency is, Tiff."

"No idea."

"E.S.P. That was the name before he even met me. It's destined, Tiff. Emerson Surveillance and Protection now features the proven resource of their very own psychic, *moi.*"

Tiffany chuckled. "When's the wedding?"

"In two weeks."

Tiffany was silent.

"You still there?"

"Taylor, you're not going to go off and get married in front of some judge or elope are you? You deserve more than that. A wedding is memories. You're your father's only daughter."

"Yeah, and he'd cough up big time, wouldn't he? I thought about that. But I couldn't deal with all the bother, and it's not important to Stone either."

Tiffany was afraid to ask, but she did anyway. "You've got everything planned, don't you?"

"Of course. It'll be simple. I'm having it in an Ethiopian restaurant. I'll have the invitations ready to go out early next week."

Tiffany closed her eyes. "Oh, Lord," she said faintly.

"Quit it, Tiffany. It's going to be great. I looked at a few books and this big wedding stuff isn't me. But I got a very good photographer and someone to videotape the whole thing for posterity."

"Good. I was just shocked at everything happening so quickly. I'm trying to absorb the fact that you've finally agreed to get married and then you tell me the wedding is so soon. Bet Stone doesn't want to take a chance on you changing your mind."

"Maybe that is it. But he doesn't have a thing to worry about. We just can't wait, Tiff. We've already made a down payment on a house."

"Taylor . . . marriage . . . a house. Goodness, I have to catch my breath."

"The house is perfect. It's a large gingerbread house with lots of room to expand for the kids."

"Kids? Are you pregnant?"

"Not yet. But folks usually get married and kids often follow."

"Taylor, marriage, a house and kids. Heavens."

"The wedding is Afrocentric. None of that European crap. And no dead white men's music either."

"I can't wait."

"I'm crazy busy with the detective agency. I thought we'd get together for dinner, but there's so much to talk about."

"Sounds good."

"All right. We'll see you around six."

Tiffany laid the phone back on the hook. "We're having dinner with Taylor and her fiancé at six this evening."

"My daughter didn't even ask to speak to me. That's typical."

"I'm sorry, Jason. She had me going so much over the news, I didn't even think about you."

"That's okay. We dads are used to it. Thank God the child is finally getting married. I'm not surprised about her wedding. Taylor hates frills. I always thought she'd elope if she ever got married at all. Having five brothers sort of jaded her with men."

"More like scared her."

"Stone Emerson is the poor soul who is going to put up with my daughter the rest of her life, right?"

"He is."

"Good. I liked him. He's a solid, decent man. He'll get her grounded."

"Or she'll have him taking flight. I'd put my money on Taylor any day. She sounds so happy, Jason."

Jason touched her hand. "Have I told you how much I appreciated your stepping into a mother's shoes for Taylor these past few years? She needed you more than you knew."

"I needed her too. She's a wonderful woman. But two weeks. I'm still in shock."

"I'm too relieved someone took her off my hands to be in shock."

Tiffany grinned. "You're terrible. But look at the time, Jason. We've got to get up."

He pulled her to him. "In twenty minutes," he whispered.

Tiffany and Jason sat in the church at his friend Marvin's wedding. Tiffany drew in her breath as she caught sight of the bride making her stately way down the aisle. The woman was very large, but she looked wonderful, as regal as any African queen and as completely feminine and lovely as any woman would want to be. She wore a crème and gold gown with a subtle African print and a matching head wrap and was accompanied by a boy beaming with pride.

She joined a tall, lean man in front of the altar with a West African outfit in similar colors of créme and gold. The traditional wedding march ceased and the church was hushed as they approached the altar.

"Beloved friends and family. We join together to witness Edna Matthews and Marvin Reynolds's covenant before God and man in the most serious and sacred union of love," the minister said. He was a man in his fifties with a wrinkled dark brown face and a mustache.

Tiffany remembered her wedding, so many years ago. A large event, very black bourgeois and European-inspired. It had been nerve-racking, the details of the fancy event far overwhelming the spiritual significance of the bond.

"In this bond, you face the future with its hopes and disappointments, it successes and failures, its pleasure and its pains, its joys and its sorrows," the minister intoned. "The future is hidden from your eyes, but these elements are mingled into a part of everyone's lives. And so, not knowing what is before you, you take each other for better or for worse, for richer or for poorer, in sickness and in health.

"If so, let us pray. Lord of life, happiness and love, bestow your grace upon this marriage and seal this covenant with your love. As you have brought them together by divine providence, sanctify them with your spirit, that they might give themselves fully one to the other and to you. Give them strength and patience to live their lives in a manner that will mutually bless them and honor your holy name through Jesus Christ our Lord. Amen."

Tiffany glanced around the church, which was simply but lushly decorated with yellow and créme roses combined with trailers of ivy. The warmth of afternoon sunshine lit up the place and she felt the presence of love, a warmth that must be the blessing of the Spirit on the simple and sacred ceremony. It contrasted starkly with her memories of the letdown she faced when she was actually before the minister in the culmination of the event her family had spent thousands of dollars and hours of anxiety on. This was it, she'd thought as she finally stood in front of the altar. It had felt like the day after Christmas. That had been it; she'd never gotten any more than that fancy wedding. But here and now, this wedding service was wholly enough and the love that suffused the room promised more to come.

The groom took his bride's hand and they faced each other. "My love," he said. "I am blessed that you will walk by my side, and we will become one. You've taught me love, laughter and true happiness. You're my best friend, the one I want to see when I wake each morning and be by my side when I sleep each night. I make a covenant to honor, respect and above all to love you for the rest of my journey through this life and forevermore."

"My love," the woman said, her rich voice filling the church. "I am blessed that you are the one whom I choose to trust, to love, and to endure whatever comes. You've taught me that it's never too late for happiness, never too late for my heart to be filled with joy, never too late for love. I make a covenant to honor, respect and above all to love you for the rest of my journey through this life and forevermore."

Tears filled Tiffany's eyes. Never too late . . .

"This celebration and ceremony," the minister said, "is the outward manifestation of a sacred and inward union of hearts that the church does bless and the state does make legal. A union created with loving purpose and kept by abiding will. Marvin Reynolds, will you have this woman to be your wedded wife and to live together in holy matrimony? Will you love her, comfort her, honor and keep her in sickness and health, in sorrow and joy, and forsaking all others, be faithful to her as long as you both shall live?"

"I do."

"Edna Matthews, will you have this man to be your wedded husband and to live together in holy matrimony? Will you love him, comfort him, honor and keep him in sickness and health, in sorrow and joy, and forsaking all others, be faithful to him as long as you both shall live?"

"I do."

"In mutual fidelity I present the rings," the minister said.

"I give you this ring as I give you my heart, and with it I wed you and pledge you my love forever." Marvin placed the ring on Edna's finger.

"I give you this ring as I give you my heart, and with it I wed you and pledge you my love forever."

"And now since you have pledged yourselves to each other in the presence of this company," the minister said, "I do, by virtue of the authority vested in me, pronounce you, Marvin Reynolds, and you, Edna Matthews, husband and wife."

As they kissed, Tiffany started to reach for Jason's hand, but instead clasped her hands together, the yearning in her own heart near to exploding. What would she give to experience a moment as deep and sacred and love-filled as the couple before her experienced? She'd made so many mistakes, followed so many wrong paths. The man she'd given her youth to had no heart to give her. And so she lost her own heart. The years and alcohol had turned her despair and loneliness into numbness. But now she was alive again and the man at her side ... She dared not hope. Was it ever too late to find your heart again?

Chapter 14

Jared spied Bennie at a table in the corner of the open-air café. She was staring into a glass of golden wine. The sun glinted off her auburn hair, giving it gold highlights. The line of her jaw was as strong as it ever was and her striking beauty undiminished, but there was a vulnerability about her that was new. A softness he could detect from yards away. Or was it his imagination? He moved toward her and she looked up.

"Have you ordered yet?"

"No, I was waiting for you."

He sat in the chair across from her as the waitress appeared. He ordered steak and soup and she ordered salad. Light fare for a heavy topic to come.

"I apologize for calling you what I did. It was unforgivable."

"I've been called worse for far less reason."

She smiled at him a little, then looked away.

"I've been thinking," Bennie said. "Maybe my father

did have something to do with the choices I made. But he didn't have everything to do with them."

"I've been thinking too. I've been with a lot of women, even thought I was in love once or twice. But I've never agreed to marry anyone."

Bennie took a sip of her wine.

"I screwed up," Jared said.

"Badly."

"What are we going to do?"

Bennie shrugged. "The wedding has been cancelled, the gifts returned. What else is there to do?"

"I suppose that's all. But I want to tell you how sorry I am. I'm not sure about what I want, and I just can't go into a marriage being ambivalent."

"We're agreed on both of your points. No way would I want to marry a man who didn't want me all the way. I thought you'd decided on your old flame Stacie."

Jared shifted in his chair. "No, it's more like she's decided on me. I went to her because I was looking for an easy way out . . ."

"Easier than coming and talking to me?" Bennie took a deep breath. "I told myself that no matter what, I was not going to get mad and go off on you, but you're trying me."

"I'm not trying to make you mad. I just want to explain myself. I got hooked into the engagement thing with Stacie too."

"Like I supposedly hooked you." Bennie drained her glass of wine and motioned to the waiter for another.

"No. It's hard to talk about because I don't understand my own self. I loved you, Bennie. Still do. I love Stacie too. But not enough to marry either of you."

Bennie got her purse and hung it over her shoulder. She stood. "You got one thing right, Jared Cates. You're one immature, pathetic son of a bitch." With those words she walked away rapidly.

The waiter brought another glass of wine and Jared picked it up. The monastery idea was starting to sound better every day. He looked at his watch. This was his designated cleanup day. He'd planned to meet with Stacie next. But he'd bungled it so badly with Bennic, he decided to put Stacie off for a few days. Geez, how did he get himself into such messes? Maybe Bennie wasn't too far off in her assessment of him.

Marvin and Edna's wedding reception was informal and filled with fun and laughter. Tiffany had soaked up every detail of décor and arrangement. Everything was very well done, although simple. The ceremony was immediately followed by a reception in the roomy church basement.

The bountiful and wonderful arrangements of crème and yellow roses and ivy must have cost a fortune. The beautiful fabric that the bride and groom had made their outfits from draped the walls, giving the room a luxurious, exotic look totally unlike a church basement. Rose-scented gold and crème candles enhanced the smell of the flowers. A bar served punch, a simple non-alcoholic sparkling grape juice, and other non-alcoholic beverages.

She could smell delicious food aromas coming from the church kitchen, and the church pianist played mellow jazzy music in the background. The buzz of conversation and laughter almost overwhelmed the music as people mingled, socialized and wished the happy couple their best wishes.

Tiffany had tried to corner Edna alone, but she was always surrounded by a group of people. She watched her from afar, fascinated by her. The woman was as old as she was and far from traditionally beautiful. She was quite a large woman with medium brown skin and comfortably pleasant features. But she shone. Her happiness, obvious confidence and self-possession had elevated her to extraordinary beauty. Tiffany almost envied her. She wanted to talk to her, get to know her. Discover her secrets. *Never too late* . . .

Jason was deep in conversation with the groom and a knot of other friends. Tiffany sipped her white grape juice. "You look as if you're worried about something." A beautiful young woman said. She was large, although not as big as the bride, but radiated the same warmth and style.

"No. I'm enjoying the reception. It was a wonderful ceremony, very moving."

"Yes. Everything's turning out well. My mother wanted to keep everything simple and on the traditional side."

"That was your mother?"

"Yes. And I just married the groom's son a few months ago."

"That's incredible. How wonderful for you both."

"By the way, my name is Carmel. Carmel Reynolds."

"I'm Tiffany Eastman." Tiffany gazed into the golden depths of her juice. "Your mother looked so happy. Sometimes getting that second chance isn't a sure bet."

"I know the feeling. This was my first marriage, but I have two older children—that was my son who gave Mama away. I had thought I had too much baggage and wasn't the type of woman who men fall in love with. But love came when and where I least expected it."

"What a blessing."

"I can't even express how much I've been blessed." She leaned to Tiffany's ear. "I just found out I'm going to have a baby. I told Steve this morning. Look at him. He can't take his eyes off me."

She nodded toward a tall, handsome man who was in a knot of men deep in some discussion. Steve's glance swept the room and landed on his wife. He smiled at her a lopsided smile full of such love Tiffany's own heart melted. Carmel gave him a little wave. "There's my honey."

"I'm here with Jason, an old friend of Marvin's from St.

Louis. He's the one in the charcoal jacket across the room with those men around the groom. Your mother's an inspiration for us older women." Tiffany continued. "I wanted to meet her, but I can't get close."

"The church ladies seem to have taken her over," Carmel said. "I'll try to get you over to her when she sits down with her plate." The waiters opened the door to the dining area where a luscious buffet spread awaited. "Let's go get a plate. I'm starving," Carmel said.

When Carmel moved through the room, heads turned. She was such a beautiful woman, Tiffany thought again. She remembered Jenny's endless diets and frowned. She wished her daughter could meet this woman who easily was twice her size and see that beauty has less to do with the body than the spirit.

Tiffany eyed the spread in appreciation, thinking that Jason's vegetarian daughter Taylor would have a stroke if she were here. Fried chicken, ribs, Virginia ham, smothered pork chops, beef brisket and more. She was going to have to roll Jason out of here once he got to all this.

They filled their plates and Carmel led her to the table where her mother sat surrounded by her matronly entourage. "Mom, I want you to meet Tiffany Eastman. She came with a friend of Marvin's."

Tiffany set her heavy plate down and proffered her hand. "I don't remember when I've been to a lovelier wedding."

Edna took her hand and smiled at her. Then her smile slowly faded. "Aren't you the Tiffany Eastman who was married to that . . . man we sent up to Congress?"

Tiffany's smile grew tighter. "The same."

"Honey, please sit down. My condolences for your loss."

"Thank you, but it's been years and I've adjusted well to my new life."

"That's good. I follow the news closely and I got the feeling that all isn't what it appears on the surface."

Tiffany's looked into Edna's intelligent, inquisitive eyes

and despite her brusqueness, she saw no hostility there. "You're right. It wasn't all that it seemed. I'm quite happy to make a new life for myself."

She felt a touch on her hand and looked up, startled. Jason was standing beside her. "I've been looking for you."

She smiled at Jason, warmth flooding her. "Let me introduce you to everybody. Have you met Edna?"

"I've had the pleasure." He took her hand with a courtly gesture and kissed it. "I've never seen Marvin look as happy."

Edna's face softened with love. "Where is he?"

"Still making the social rounds. He'll be in here in a moment." Then he looked toward the buffet. "Save me a place honey, I'm going to get a plate."

Edna looked toward one of the women. "Would you get me and Marvin plates? I know he's hungry too." The church ladies fluttered off and Tiffany and Carmel sat at the table. "Jason seems like a good man. Marvin tells me they've been good friends for years. It seems like he's making you feel pretty good. Is that so?"

Tiffany was taken aback by the woman's directness. "Yes, very much so," she finally answered.

"We'll be friends," Edna said.

Tiffany knew it was so. She liked this direct, confident woman. It seemed as if she gained the facility of recognizing a friend at first sight and they recognized her also. Tiffany wished love were as simple. "Yes, we'll be friends," she said to Edna.

Chapter 15

"You're not hungry? You knew you were coming here for dinner," Taylor said.

"You should have seen the buffet at the wedding, Taylor. It would have made any carnivore's mouth water, and Jason and I are guilty of digging in. But you and Stone eat."

"Please do," Jason said. "I need to sit on the sofa and digest my food for a while anyway. You got any Pepto-Bismol in here, Taylor?"

She nodded toward the bathroom and Jason left the room. "Well, I guess Stone and I will go ahead and eat. I made stuffed green peppers."

"What did you stuff them with, baby?" Stone asked.

"Brown rice, seaweed and adzuki beans."

"Oh."

"It doesn't taste as bad as it sounds," Taylor said.

"You're not marrying her for her cooking, I hope," Jason said, returning to the room with a large pink bottle.

"No. That's definitely not what I'm marrying her for," Stone said with a grin. "Fortunately, we eat out a lot."

"A plate Carmel fixed for us is in the car. Ribs, fried chicken . . ." Jason said.

Stone's eyes gleamed, then he shot a guilty glance toward Taylor.

"Go ahead and eat it," she said. "Just leaves more stuffed peppers for me."

"Here's the keys, son. It's the silver Jeep Cherokee with the rental tag in the back," Jason said.

Stone looked taken aback at the word son, then a slow, sweet grin worked its way across his face. He dipped his head a little and went down to the car.

"Stone grew up without a father. He has two sisters and his mother was a single parent. He's probably never heard anyone call him son before," Taylor observed.

"Got to start sometime," Jason said. "Got a spoon for this?" he shook the pink bottle.

An hour later, after Stone had eaten and Jason had recovered from his indigestion, Jason took Stone out to "get to know his new son better" as he put it. Tiffany and Taylor curled up on the sofa, sipping herb tea. Tiffany looked around the apartment, feeling a pang of nostalgia. "So many changes in such a short time."

"Life is like a river, Tiff. It rushes on, sometimes placid, sometimes a torrent, but you can't stop the forward motion."

"Sometimes, I wish I knew where I was going."

"Ah, that's the question. I see flashes and glimpses of the road ahead. It's a tough one for you, but you'll be all right."

"Did I ever tell you that your psychic stuff gives me the willies?" Tiffany said. "We want to know the future, yet we don't. I think we fear that once we know what's going to happen, it's carved in stone, immutable."

"Yes. We want control over our destinies. People only want to know the specifics. Does he love me? Should I change jobs?"

"You've always known you were psychic. Over years of knowing you, I saw that in many instances it's true. How much do you really see, Taylor?"

"Not much. It's as if the future is veiled by a curtain that blows aside at intervals. Sometimes it's difficult to interpret what you see. I see difficulties ahead for you, but I see happiness also. Pleasure and pain. But I couldn't give you specifics. Even if I did, since I don't know the context, it would be meaningless."

"So I'd be wasting my money on a psychic hotline?"

"Exactly."

Tiffany pondered this for a while, feeling the pull to question Taylor about her future anyway and the dread of knowing. Her bottom line was that if she couldn't change it, she really didn't want to know.

"I had a dream," Taylor said.

Tiffany looked up. Taylor's dreams were always interesting.

"I dreamed I was getting married. The ceremony was totally awesome and different from anything I've ever experienced. I did some research and realized I was remembering a prior life."

"I was where Ethiopia is located now. I was a member of the ruling class and I was getting married. I wanted some features of that wedding."

"You're re-enacting an ancient Ethiopian princess fantasy? The only thing you have in common with the culture is your skin color."

"They are my ancestors. I know it. Recent ancestors. Unlike most blacks in America, I have a recent bloodline that isn't West African, but East African. My name was Millette back then. It has meaning for me, and Stone agrees. I'm having an Ethiopian wedding."

"So . . ." Tiffany started to say, but Taylor interrupted her.

"It's at the Blue Nile Ethiopian restaurant. They're catering, too."

"What time are you thinking about?"

"The usual. Saturday late afternoon will be good for the ceremony, and we can do sort of a continuous buffet dinner instead of a sit-down one," Taylor said.

"It sounds good."

"It will be. Now that I've filled you in on the wedding arrangements, I want to hear about you and Dad. Hot stuff, huh?"

Tiffany was speechless.

"You have a glow about you, but I can also see that it's eating you up—this love thing." Taylor patted her hand. "Don't worry, it's always hard at first when you're not sure, but it will work out."

Tiffany withdrew her hand. "Taylor, you know I love you, but I'm not comfortable discussing my relationship with your father with you."

Taylor sighed. "Fair enough. I'll drop it, but it's so juicy. I'm dying to know—"

"Taylor."

"Okay." Taylor hugged her suddenly. "You've always been more than a mom to me. I'm so happy for you, Tiff."

Tiffany touched her cheek. "I'm happy too. For both you and me."

"I'll have diet Coke, thank you," Tiffany said to the stewardess.

She took a sip out of the glass the stewardess handed her and glanced over at Jason, who was engrossed in a magazine. The wedding was wonderful and she had thoroughly enjoyed meeting Jason's friends, but . . . the wedding had touched a place inside her that she thought she'd locked away. The place where she desired, craved, needed the things most women wanted. A man to love who cherished her. Security. Someone to grow old with. A tall order and far too many women weren't getting it.

Was she hoping too much to think she could be one of the lucky ones?

"Did you have a good time?" Jason's soft words interrupted her thoughts.

"I did."

He took her hand. "I enjoy having you stay with me. No. Enjoy is not the right word. I want you to stay with me."

Tiffany's heart felt like it was going to jump out of her chest.

"Say yes. Say you won't move out."

"What are you asking me, Jason?"

"I want you to consider Diana's home your home now."

A pause. She didn't think Jason could have worded it in a worse way. Not only did he not ask the question every woman wants to hear from the man she loves, but also he said the words "Diana's home."

"I hear what you're saying, Jason. I don't plan to move out anytime soon. But you asked me to make Diana's home my home. I don't want Diana's home or Diana's man or Diana's place in your heart. I want my own."

Jason looked surprised, then dismayed. "I didn't mean it like it sounded," he stammered.

Tiffany sighed. "I know, honey." She patted his hand and he relaxed a little.

About half an hour later, Tiffany looked at her watch. It was after eleven and Jason was dozing. Most passengers had their headphones on, were engrossed in the news or dozing. She slipped off her pump and ran her foot up under Jason's pants leg. He raised his head instantly and raised an eyebrow. "I want you," she mouthed silently.

She got up and headed toward the restroom. She locked the door and stared in the mirror. The seconds ticked past. Three taps, a pause, another tap. She smiled, opened the door and let him in.

The alarm clock shrieked and Jason turned it off. They both groaned in unison. They'd gotten in from the airport late and fell into bed exhausted. She sure didn't want to face Monday. Jason was stumbling toward the shower already and she turned over and shut her eyes. A few minutes more . . .

Jason was gently shaking her awake. "Tiff. Time to get up." She groaned again, but got up and headed to the shower. She could live for a long time without Mondays and this was a doozy.

Hours later, on her way home from work, she considered again what it was about Monday that was so hellacious. It stayed Monday all day and every blessed thing that could go wrong did, starting with Moira calling in sick. Tiffany pulled through the Boston Market drive-through to pick up a meal. She knew neither she nor Jason would feel like cooking tonight.

When she pulled up to the house, she frowned at the strange car in the driveway. She was certainly not up for company. Was Jason home yet? When she opened the garage, his car wasn't there. She parked, got out and turned to go see who was in the car, when she heard her daughter cry out, "Mom." she embraced her enthusiastically.

Jenny pulled back and studied her face. "I will assume you are happy to see me deep inside, but you look beat, Mom."

"I am. We got in from Atlanta late last night. What are you doing here, baby? I thought you were coming out later in the summer?"

"I changed my mind. I thought I'd come out earlier. Jason said I was welcome anytime."

"It's wonderful to see you." She bent to get the food out of the car. "Are you hungry?"

"Not really. I got something when I hit the city. You didn't tell me what you thought of my new car."

Tiffany peered out of the garage door at the white Honda Accord. "Nice choice. I like it." She pressed the button to close the garage door. "Let's go in."

Jenny trailed her. "So Mom, what's the setup here, really? Are you still looking for your own apartment or are you settling into this big house?"

"So far I'm settling in."

"Hmmmmmm. And how is that?"

A tinge of irritation touched her. All she wanted was to get a bite to eat, take a hot bath and sink into bed. "Let me show you Taylor's old room. You can stay there."

Jenny shot her a glance, but thankfully decided to let her line of questioning slide. "Where is the AA meeting tonight?" she asked.

Tiffany would prefer that she continue on in her former vein rather than get going on that topic. "I have no idea. Jenny, I'm going to get a bite to eat, then I'm going to take a bath and lie down. Make yourself at home. Jason will probably be in shortly, but I'm really very tired. We got in very late from Atlanta last night. It's been a long day."

"I understand, Mom. It was an impulse move and I thought I'd surprise you."

"I'm happy to see you, it's just that—"

Jenny raised a hand. "I understand," she repeated.

Tiffany fixed herself a plate from the take-out food she left on the stove.

"Do Jason's sons drop by very often?" Jenny asked with studied casualness.

Tiffany's hand paused. She visualized Jenny among Jason's sons and wondered if it would be like letting a chicken loose in a roomful of cocks. Jason had five very attractive, eligible sons with only one married and one engaged, maybe. Jenny had changed. There was a confidence about her lately that Tiffany bet was very attractive to men. A don't-give-a-damn attitude combined with the hint of quickly combustible sexuality and that male energy that many men seemed to find attractive.

"I don't see Jason's sons that often. Things have been going so fast, sometimes it seems as if I just got here. I haven't had a chance to get to know his children as well as I'd like."

A fleeting look of disappointment crossed Jenny's face. "Okay. I'm going to bring my bags in and get settled. I planned to go a meeting tonight."

Tiffany ate and lay down on the bed. She heard Jason come in and the rise and fall of Jason and Jenny's voices. She wondered what they were talking about. But she couldn't force herself to get up and soon felt herself sinking into the deep, black velvet of sleep. She felt rather than heard Jason join her and gave a contented murmur.

Thank God it was Friday, Tiffany thought as she stood in the kitchen chopping onions for dinner. The week had drained her reserves. Jenny had gone to an Alcoholics Anonymous meeting every single night of the week, extending an invitation for Tiffany to join her at every meeting, often right in front of Jason. If her daughter wanted to live in her past for the rest of her life that was her business, but Tiffany resented being dragged into it. Those days were over and she was trying to build a new life on fragile foundations with a new man. She didn't need the stress of his being constantly reminded . . .

She shook off the anxiety. The phone rang and Tiffany took her time getting to it. She'd bet money it was for Jenny. An astonishing number of men were calling for her already. Jenny seemed to love it, allowing them to wine and dine her in the few days since she'd been there, but taking no one seriously. Tiffany marveled over the men trailing her daughter as if she were a dog in heat. The phone stopped ringing, but then the doorbell rang. Tiffany wiped her hands off with a towel and went to answer it.

A pretty girl stood framed in the doorway. *She must be a friend of Jenny's,* Tiffany thought.

"Is Jared here?" she asked.

"No, this is his father's home."

"He asked me to meet him here." She glanced at her watch. "Maybe I'm a little early."

"Please come in," Tiffany said. "Would you like something to drink?"

"Ummmm, no thank you."

"Why don't you come into the kitchen with me? I'm getting dinner on."

"Sure."

"By the way, my name is Tiffany Eastman."

"I'm Stacie Veach."

Tiffany's eyebrows shot up and she darted a glance at the girl's left hand. No ring yet.

Tiffany put the onions in butter to fry and opened the refrigerator, taking out a pitcher of iced tea. "Sure you don't want something to drink? I'm having a glass of tea."

"That would be nice if you're having one." Stacie glanced at her watch again.

"What time were you expecting Jared?"

"About fifteen minutes from now. I'm early."

Tiffany poured their tea and sat down at the table across from Stacie. "I warn you the tea is Southern style, very sweet."

The girl nodded and gave her a small smile. Tiffany could see a slight tremor in her hand as she reached for the tea.

"You seem a little nervous."

Stacie started and glanced at her watch again. "I am.

I've done something, and I'm happy I did it, but I'm anxious about the outcome."

"Oh?"

"Do you know Benita?"

Tiffany's eyes widened and she set her tea down carefully. "You're speaking about the girl Jared was engaged to? I've met her briefly."

"Jared said he was going to marry me. But he's been ducking and dodging me for almost a week. I think he's still seeing her. He has to choose between us once and for all!"

"So what did you do?" Tiffany asked.

"Jared's supposed to get here in a few minutes and then I asked Benita to show up right after. She said she would. He's going to have to choose. Me or her, here and now."

Uh-oh, Tiffany thought. She was definitely staying out of this one.

Chapter 16

The doorbell rang and Stacie flinched. "I'll go get it," Tiffany said. She shook her head. She hoped it was Jared, but he had a key and didn't usually ring the bell. She pulled open the door and Benita stood there.

"I got a message that Jared was here and he wanted to talk to me?" she said.

"I left that message." Stacie's voice rang out.

"What are *you* doing here?" Benita asked.

Tiffany pivoted. "Why don't you women come in, sit down and talk things over—"

"I told you the truth," Stacie said to Benita. "Jared does have something to say to you, to both of us. He told me he would give me a ring and he's been ducking and dodging ever since. I was told you two were seen together. He needs to make a choice. I'm not putting up with this a second longer."

"You don't have to. Jared and I are through. I'm out of here." Benita wheeled and walked out into the front drive toward her car.

Stacie took off after her, grabbed her shoulder and wheeled her around. "No, we're not through. I want to talk to you."

Benita knocked Stacie's hand away. "Take your hands off me. Since I don't have the desperate need for a man like you do, I don't see any reason we have to talk."

"You've got some nerve calling me desperate, you man-stealing . . . wench!"

Tiffany walked out onto the front porch more slowly and eyed the girls squaring off. She had no idea what she would do if they got into a catfight on Jason's front lawn.

Right then Jared pulled up. Jenny walked out from the back of the house toward his car. He got out slowly, his eyes on Stacie and Benita who were still arguing.

When he slammed his door shut, their heads turned toward him. They both started to move toward him. Then they saw Jenny and they stopped as if they'd slammed into a brick wall.

Jenny had on skintight leopard pants and a black leather halter top-like contraption. She oozed glamour and sexuality. She moved toward Jared and he whispered something, and she lifted her head. Both of the watching women gasped as he kissed Jenny passionately. He gave neither of them a second look as he opened his car door for Jenny, got into the other side and drove away.

Both women looked after his car with their mouths hanging open. Tiffany was aghast herself. She had no idea that Jenny knew Jared that well.

Benita spoke first. "Son of a bitch," she said.

Stacie shook her head. "I guess you were right. You and I don't have a thing to talk about. I've been played like a fool by that man."

"Don't feel too bad about it," Benita murmured. "You're not the only one."

* * *

Later that evening, Jason carefully laid out the fancy white Ethiopian outfit with multicolored embroidery that Tiffany had bought him for Taylor's wedding. He felt as though the walls of the room were closing in on him, as if he were suffocating. He sat heavily on the bed. What did Tiffany want from him? He'd told her that he wanted her to stay with him, to share the house he'd shared with . . . Diana.

Diana wouldn't begrudge her home. She had been sweet and loving, and as strange and fey as his daughter Taylor. She'd laugh. *I see you finally got some, old man. It's about time.*

He buried his face in his hands. His Diana. Thirty years and he still missed her, could hear her voice. But her features were fading away. Her face was as misty as the ghost she'd become. His fault, his entire fault she died. He was a doctor, for God's sake. He should have insisted that the birth take place in the hospital instead of the fancy notions of home births with the soothing warmth of water.

He should have been able to save her. All his fancy medical school training had been for naught as she and his newborn daughter slipped away from him. Jason tried to catch the sob in his throat, but it escaped him, soon followed by another and another. His fault. All his fault.

"Oh, Jason." Tiffany was there beside him and she cradled him in her arms. He fought for control, regained it. Deeply ashamed, he turned his head away from her.

"It's all right, baby," she crooned. She lay down and pulled him close to her gently and murmured soft words of comfort. She was too much of a woman to ask the questions a younger female would—what's wrong? Tell me what's the matter. She knew better. His Tiffany. He didn't want to do without her, but he was afraid.

Sometimes the one you love the most leaves you alone forever.

It was a while later when he finally spoke. "It's because of her. My ex-wife Diana. Remembering . . . how she died. It was terrible. I killed her, Tiffany. I killed her and my little baby."

He glanced at her face and her eyes were wide ovals of sympathy and pain.

"I put her through hell so I could finish medical school, so I could make my own dreams come true. Then I did and I finally started my internship." He rolled over on his back. "I should have insisted she go to the hospital. She had five births. I should have known of her weakness."

Tiffany was silent, but her arms tightened around him. "How can I deserve love and happiness when hers was ripped away from her? She loved her children so much. She loved me. She loved life. She was a wonderful woman. A perfect woman."

He looked at Tiffany, willing her to say something— anything. He wanted to get mad. He wanted her to rip him to shreds and make him feel like dirt. He wanted to feel anything other than this too familiar anguish of loss and guilt that thirty years hadn't dulled.

"I'm sorry, Jason," was all she said.

"Diana should be here to see her only daughter marry."

"You're right, she should. It's very sad."

"If Taylor had the steady hand of a mother, she wouldn't be so scattered. I did the best I could."

"You did."

He gathered her into his arms. "Don't ever leave me, Tiffany. Promise me you won't."

She murmured soft words, and melting into him, offering the gift of her loving, her body, her warmth and her life. He needed her so much and that was a fearful thing for him too.

* * *

Later, much later, after sweet and soulful lovemaking, Tiffany watched Jason's chest rise and fall with the even rhythm of sleep. He'd asked her never to leave him, to share his home and his life. What had she waited to hear? *Grow old with me, be my partner, be my wife.* She wanted papers on the man. She wanted the hallowed position his sainted first wife had.

Maybe, just maybe, if he could work through the old ghost of his past, he'd realize that he wanted the same thing she did. But she couldn't shake the fear. Maybe she wanted too much. Maybe she wasn't good—she stopped the thought. Of course she was good enough for any man. No matter what her abusive husband had told her. Had showed her. Had beaten into her.

Tiffany squeezed her eyes shut and willed sleep, but it eluded her. She was not a young woman. She'd been around the block more than once and she knew sometimes a person had to be satisfied with what life offered. Expectations of more only sowed seeds of unhappiness. He tossed in his sleep and spooned his warm body around hers. She never wanted to have to do without this man, and with God's grace, maybe she wouldn't have to.

"Did you see the look on those women's faces?" Jenny asked Jared with a grin.

"To be frank, I was too occupied with you to notice them, and afterward I was hauling butt to get out of there before either of them got to me and lynched me or something."

"We weren't being too mean pulling that trick on them?"

A frown touched Jared's face. "It was an impulse. Not

as much mean as cowardly on my part. I feel bad about not talking to Stacie first."

"You can always tell her we didn't mean anything by the kiss, that it was for effect only."

"I doubt if she'll believe me. It's just that I've had enough of emotional confrontations with women. Thank God you picked up the phone when I called the house to have someone tell Stacie I'd be late. I could hardly believe it when you told me that those two had got together to ambush me."

"You'd better thank God I'm so nosy."

"And an eavesdropper."

"That too." Jenny stretched a little against the leather seats of his car and Jared looked sideways at her. She was one hot-looking woman. He'd been having a pleasant conversation with her when she'd heard the doorbell and asked him to hold on while she checked out Stacie. She'd heard Stacie set up an ambush with Benita and given him the 4-1-1.

Then they set up this little scheme. He'd been so angry at Stacie and Benita, he'd been more than willing. He wanted to meet with Stacie to tell her that the engagement wasn't happening. He'd picked his father's house for moral backbone and witnesses to his possible murder. Why did she always have to drag Benita into it?

When he'd seen Jenny walk across the lawn, she looked so good, he'd almost had a heart attack. He'd met her in passing before, but he'd never really noticed her until now. She looked like a pixieish Halle Berry, all warm and honey-colored. She oozed confidence and sex appeal. And when he kissed her—he'd been upset and anxious, but the sweetness of her lips soon made him forget his two ex-fiancées and possible mother-in-law gawking at him.

He felt a little crazy, a little wild, and he wanted to kiss her again more than anything. "Want to come by my place? I'll cook dinner," he asked.

"No, actually I have plans. Do you mind dropping me off at a friend's house?"

A pang of disappointment mixed with a touch of disbelief struck him. He wasn't used to a woman turning down his invitations so casually.

"Maybe later?"

She smiled at him. "Maybe. But I've been awfully busy since I've gotten to St. Louis. So many new things to do. I'm sure I'll see you around the house once in a while. Oh, turn right here. It's down two blocks to your right."

A minute later she was getting out of his car. A quick smile and wriggle of her fingers and she was gone. He felt dismissed. It wasn't a pleasant feeling. He was used to women lighting up around him, responding positively to his slightest move. This woman had him off balance and he didn't like the feeling. Once he cleaned up the mess he was in now, he was going to turn his attentions to Ms. Jenny Eastman.

Chapter 17

"You never told me what's going on between you and Jared," Tiffany said to Jenny as they sat in the kitchen snapping green beans for dinner.

"Not a thing."

"He's over here a lot more since you started staying here. He's quite disappointed you're home so seldom."

Jenny snapped a bean and shrugged. "Mom, you know what type of man Jared is?"

"No, I don't."

"He's a dog. He's the type of man who has had women sniffing after him his entire life."

"I thought you told me you thought he was fine."

"He's too fine for his own good. But do you see how much I've changed since the days I was chasing after that man, Brent, who didn't want me?"

"I sure do. And I must say it's for the better. You're oozing confidence and I notice that it's you all the dogs are sniffing after now."

"And I don't give them the time of day. The next time

I fall in love it's going to be with someone worth me, not some guy who can't handle his women, like Jared."

"I think he feels bad. There's something inside him that's afraid to settle down and commit, although I think intellectually he feels it's time. At least that's what his dad says."

"Whatever. But I'm a player-hater now. In fact, I can't stand the type of men who go after women who don't give them the time of day. Sad thing is that sometimes it seems like that's ninety-seven percent of the male population. If I acted like I was interested in him, he'd string me along and snap me off in a second."

Tiffany looked at her daughter with a worried eye. "Don't snap back too much in the opposite direction. Sometimes you have to give men time before you can see what they're really made of. And I hope you don't toy with Jared or his feelings."

"Don't you see that I'm leaving Jared alone? Although it is a temptation to dog him as much as he's probably dogged a whole lot of women."

"When you talk like this, you sound bitter."

"I'm not bitter, Mom. Just realistic."

Tiffany had nothing to say to that. The phone broke the ensuing silence and Tiffany moved across the kitchen to answer it. "Dante!"

"It's your brother," she whispered to Jenny.

"I'm going to be able to bring the baby to Taylor's wedding, but Celeste has to work. She can't come," he said.

"That's too bad, but I'm thrilled to see you and little Dante."

"Take care of yourself, okay? See you next week."

"Love you."

"Ditto."

Tiffany replaced the phone on the hook, feeling excited

that she was going to see her son and beloved grandson so soon again. She'd give a lot to be able to live in the same city with them.

"Dante's doing great," Jenny said.

"Ever since he married, he's a new man."

"I like Celeste. She's sweet, but down-to-earth too. Bro did good. I'm especially glad he's doing so well now because he had it harder than me in a lot of ways."

"Why do you say that?"

"Dad never treated me like he did Dante. You never saw a lot of what he used to say to him because he knew you'd take Dante's part. He'd go on and on about how sorry he was. I never saw anything worse about Dante than any other guy, but it was like Dad hated him or something."

Tiffany bit her lip. She had a lot of guilt over what Dante went through growing up and it made her satisfaction and pride in the man he'd become even stronger. "Ever since his father died, he's coming into his own. So are you," Tiffany added. "I'm pleased with the way you're handling your life. You've come back from some trials that would have pounded many young women down and kept them that way."

"I work on it every single day. That's why it disturbs me to see how much you've let your recovery slip. It's an ongoing process. So is coming to peace with the past. It's not an instant process. You went through years of hell, Mom."

Tiffany shrugged. "Sometimes I feel that people put far too much emphasis on the past. We live in the present and that's all that counts or matters."

Jenny dropped her eyes. "You should see the West African outfit I got to wear to Taylor's wedding, matching head wrap and all. It's fabulous," she said.

*   *   *

"Taylor, if you don't stand still, I'm going to stick this pin straight into your butt," Kara said as she pinned the sash over Taylor's gown.

"I can't believe I'm actually going to do it. I'm going to get married." A look of panic filled Taylor's eyes.

"Yes, you are. It's far too late to back out now."

"That's not what Jared thought."

"Somebody needs to take a cane to Jared's hide."

"Are you about ready?" Tiffany called, sticking her head into the room and looking at her watch.

"Twenty more minutes," Kara said to Tiffany. "I give up on this sash. I think it looks better with it off anyway," she muttered.

Kara circled Taylor. "You look great, girl. At first I didn't know about these gowns you chose, but they are fabulous and yours is the bomb."

They were made of flowing white cotton and edged with intricate embroidery of primary colors.

"Thank you, Ms. Matron of Honor."

They smiled at each other.

"C'mon. Let me see what I can do with those dreadlocks," Kara said.

"What did you have in mind?"

"Upswept with those flowers weaved through." Taylor looked over at the small, brightly colored blooms.

"Sounds good."

Kara picked up Taylor's dreads and started to twine them into an intricate pattern.

"Lord, I can't believe that you're getting married. Brent lost the bet."

"He should have known better than to bet against you."

"That's what I think, but you can't tell a man anything."

"How's Stone holding up?"

"Somewhat bemused. I think the wedding plans surprised him. He had a more traditional wedding in mind. A traditional wedding march, bride in white, flowers, etc."

I'm in white. And he knows I'm not hearing any Wagner in a marriage ceremony of mine. He'll be pleasantly surprised. It will seem familiar to him."

"How so?"

"We've married before. Many times. This is his favorite ceremony. He's my twin flame."

"Oh. Why do you always say something outrageous like that just to have the last word?"

"What are you talking about, 'just to have the last word'? I'm telling the truth."

"You need to quit."

"Haven't we had this conversation before?" Taylor asked.

"Regularly."

"Kara, I love you. You're the sister I never had."

"I love you too. Now be still while I get these flowers set in your hair right."

The music was definitely different, with Middle Eastern overtones, but it was pleasant. A warm feeling enveloped Tiffany as she watched Taylor's traditional western entrance and processional, preceded by her many diverse looking bridesmaids. White, black, Hispanic, all shapes, sizes and ages, that was like Taylor. Tiffany had been to too many weddings where the bridesmaids all appeared to be fashioned out of the same mold.

They all tried to step to the beat, but the music didn't have much of a beat, so they couldn't quite manage it, the poor things. A male singer was wailing in an unidentifiable language, whatever Ethiopians speak, she supposed, accompanied by the twangs and bellows of similarly unidentifiable instruments. The singer's voice soared up into something like a screech and half the bridesmaids flinched.

The celebration would be a blend of things that Taylor

stamped with her own brand of uniqueness. When Taylor had leaves delivered instead of flowers, Tiffany threw up her hands. But she admitted the leaves did look good. The restaurant had been transformed into something reminiscent of a tropical forest, with the lush greenery that gave off a fragrant, vibrant green scent.

Unusual would probably be the word the attendees would use to describe the wedding. But Tiffany was sure it was a wedding that would be remembered, and wasn't that what really counted?

"Children of God, welcome." The officiator of the marriage vows was a self-styled Egyptian priestess. Tiffany prayed she wouldn't feel called on to sacrifice something. Taylor had mentioned that might be a possibility.

"Please stand and kneel and together we may call upon the gods to gather and bless this momentous occasion."

Something like a collective groan whispered through the guests at either the thought of getting on the floor or the word "god" in the plural and decidedly uncapitalized.

"I am not getting on this hard floor with my arthritis," a querulous voice cried out from the back. The priestess hesitated. "You may all stand then."

Tiffany looked at Taylor to see if she was horrified, but she looked like she was going to crack up with laughter. The poor groom, Stone, looked slightly horrified, but that's what he got for doing the typical male thing of letting the women handle all the wedding details. Stone was no fool and he knew Taylor was a trip.

"Raise your arms to the gods and cry to the winds for their blessings," the priestess cried. Apparently the gods had a taste for jazzy Grover Washington music, because that's what came on while the priestess gyrated and danced before the altar. Many of the guests, who were mostly Taylor's friends after all, decided to join the dancing when the music changed to some vintage George Duke funk.

"Let me have a witness," the priestess cried.

"Yes, Lord!" was the congregation's reply.

Ahhh, this would be quite a wedding, Tiffany thought.

Now, why couldn't he have a daughter who would have a wedding full of shades of pink and white roses, maybe a little Mendelssohn and all the traditional frills he was accustomed to? He would have been more than happy to pay for it, Jason thought.

After they'd finally gotten the guests calmed down, he had to admit the ceremony was full of meaning and beauty and the vows they had written to one another were moving. But now . . . he stretched out his long legs from the cross-legged position he'd assumed for the past hour. Were the belly dancers really necessary? And the music. He rubbed his temples. Weird Middle Eastern music alternated with classic soul and eighties funk. He guessed he could be happy there was no rap.

He reached out and broke off a bit of the soft injera bread with his hand. No forks, no knifes. Everybody had to sit on the floor and eat with their fingers. And since he didn't ordinarily frequent Ethiopian restaurants, it was like nothing he'd ever experienced before. But the food was good. Taylor had loosened up, and fragrant stews with chicken and lamb were served along with plenty of vegetarian dishes. He scooped up a bit of stew with the bread. Doro wat, it was called. He'd have to try to get the recipe.

A new tune blared from the speakers. "Atomic Dog." He remembered that song from when his sons were young and he'd gotten so sick of it he'd been blessedly happy when it had died out in popularity. The belly dancers stopped shaking their bellies and started shaking their rumps. Many of the guests remembered the song also and jumped up from the floor and joined the belly dancers in the general rump-shaking. It was past ten and Taylor and Stone had long since left for their honeymoon. They were spending the night in a New York hotel before taking off across the Atlantic to Egypt and East Africa. The party showed no signs of abating, and Jason's head and rump were sore from the assaults of both the music and sitting on the floor. He turned to Tiffany, but she was getting up.

"Wanna dance?" she asked.

What he wanted to do was groan, but he heaved himself up off the floor and followed her to at least bob his head up and down to the pounding beat. Jason Cates, the good sport.

"C'mon, shake it, Dad," Donovan cried out. The boy had obviously had too much Ethiopian honey-wine to drink. Jason was not in the habit of shaking anything, at least not in public. Parliament Funkadelic wailed, *Why must I feel like that? Why must I chase the cat? Nothing but the dog in me.* The eternal question and the profound answer. He looked down at Tiffany. She could shake it very well. He added that to his list of her admirable traits. He couldn't wait to get out of there and be alone with her.

"Great wedding, Mom," Dante said. "Uh, can I have my baby back? We need to get back home."

"Surely you're not planning to stay up late driving? You should get a hotel." Tiffany nuzzled little Dante's neck and luxuriated in the delicious smell of baby.

"It's not that far to Charlotte. I want to get home to Celeste tomorrow before it's too late. We have plans."

"You should have flown."

"The short distance to Atlanta? You jest."

"Okay," Tiffany reluctantly handed the baby over.

"Don't fret, Mom. For those unaccustomed to it, this Ethiopian coffee renders anyone who drinks it incapable of sleeping for at least the next twenty-four hours. I'll pull into Charlotte barely after midnight. I usually stay up until then anyway."

"You've made up your mind. You were always stubborn. Come here." She pulled him and the baby close to her and hugged them fiercely. "I love you, you hear? Take care. I plan to see more of you, Dante. The family you are building is . . . it's wonderful. You turned out to be a man. More of a man than your father ever could conceive, and I'm proud of you."

He kissed her cheek gently. "I love you too, Mom. Take care of that new man you've got. He's a keeper." He shifted the baby on his other hip. "This little guy will sleep all the way. I'll call you tomorrow."

"I'll be waiting," Tiffany said. She watched her son walk away holding his child. She'd meant what she'd said from the depths of her heart. He hadn't had an example of how to be a man like Jason's sons had, but he was the equal of any of them. She was so proud of him it hurt.

She had so many regrets. Regrets she hadn't made sure he had a happier childhood and protected him better. Her regrets were turning to ashes as the reality of the good things in the present came into focus. She was finally able to accept the past, accept that she had done the best she could and lay it to rest. What remained was a happy extended family, and it was all good.

Chapter 18

An alarm or a siren broke into the dark grayness of Jason's slumber. An uneasy dream. Must be a warning of some sort.

"Jason," Tiffany's soft, sleep-filled voice said by his ear. "Answer that."

He reached out to pick up the phone, stilling it midring and turning on the light nearly simultaneously. "Yes?" He listened for a moment. Tiffany struggled up. *Was it Dante? Oh, God let it not be about Dante.*

"Yes, she's here," Jason said. His voice was full of jagged edges. He handed Tiffany the phone and her face picked up the shadow of fear from his.

"Mom," Jenny's voice was husky. Tiffany's hand tightened on the receiver. "Dante was in an accident. They said he was all right but . . . but little Dante is dead. Oh, God. And that's not all. He was drinking, Mom. Dante was drinking."

A black wall slammed her. Hard obsidian slamming into

her again and again. Little Dante was dead and he was over and done. Over and done. Over. Done.

And Dante had been drinking. He'd killed his own son. Somehow she'd infected her perfect happy Dante, and all she'd believed about him had been a lie. She was a lie herself, worthless. A loathsome plague. Her sickness had infected Dante and cost her grandson his life.

God, God, God, why have you forsaken me? Terrible and cruel God, kill me. Please have mercy and kill me because I can't bear this knowledge.

She waited for death, willed it, prayed for it incoherently.

It didn't come.

She came back to herself and stared into Jason's wet eyes. "It's not true, is it?"

Jason said nothing.

"Answer me, dammit," she screamed. She pounded his chest with her fists, fury filling her and overtaking the pain. He caught her hands and tried to draw her close. She struggled but wasn't strong enough to break free from him to lash out.

"Oh, no. Oh, no," she moaned. But how could she tell her anguish to this man she loved? Reveal the blackness inside her?

She pulled away. She lay back on the bed and drew her knees up, curling into the tiniest fetal ball possible. She had to be dead too, because she couldn't live with everything she believed and important to her turned to ashes. Ashes.

Jason had made the calls. They were leaving for Charlotte. Tiffany had withdrawn into herself and her pain. He prayed that he could be there for her, and he wrapped his fingers around hers. At least her son was alive although the loss of her grandson was a tragedy. He was afraid to tell her what he'd been told about Dante—that he was a fugitive, that he'd walked away from the hospital. Nobody had been able to locate him.

When they arrived at Dante's house in Charlotte, a small, brown woman with her wig askew and a harried look on her face met them. "I'm Celeste's mother, Lucille," she said.

Jason watched Tiffany mouth pleasantries that didn't show in her eyes. Her face was still frozen, her eyes dead and dry.

The woman blew her nose. "I came by to give you the keys to the house. Celeste tried to kill herself."

Tiffany's eyes focused on her. "Is she all right?" she asked.

"She's in the hospital. The police came and told her and stayed with her while she called family."

"Why wasn't Dante with her when they told her about her son?" Tiffany asked.

The woman looked at her sharply. "You don't know Dante is missing?"

"What?" Tiffany sank into a chair and leaned on Jason for support.

He should have told her, he thought. Better that than to learn like this.

"Tell me what are you talking about," she demanded.

"Dante rode with his son in the ambulance. Little Dante was pronounced dead. As soon as everybody's back was turned, he just got up and walked out of the hospital, away from his dead baby and away from his wife. He walked away before they were able to test his blood for alcohol, but everyone knew he was drunk. He's a wanted man now, and deservedly so." Celeste's mother's eyes were pools of resentment and anger.

Tiffany covered her face with her hands and he felt her tremble. She slowly raised her head and whispered as if to herself, "I'm sorry. I had no idea."

"They said Celeste cried a little when they told her, but

they thought she'd be fine," the woman continued. "She told them her sister lived down the street and she was on her way. She said she'd prefer it if they left. They left. Then she got every pill bottle in the house and lined them up in front of her and started taking the pills one by one. The house was dark when we got there. Her daddy thought she had left to go to the hospital already, but I just knew she was in there. We broke a window and . . . we found her. We got her to a hospital in time and they pumped her stomach."

"She is alive," Tiffany whispered.

"She'll be all right. Physically at least. Her doctor recommended that we put her in a mental hospital for a while . . . She told me some things. I knew there were problems with the marriage, but I had no idea the extent."

"I didn't know, Jason," Tiffany whispered to him. Her eyes swam with pain and tears. She stood on unsteady legs. "I need to be alone for a while." She walked toward the bathroom.

The sun shone bright, hot and yellow. God was too cruel to allow anything but sunshine on the day she buried her grandson. She leaned on Jason's strong arm as he led her into the funeral home and shut her eyes at the sight of the small casket. It was covered with white gladioli. From now on, she would associate grief and death with gladioli, and she was glad they picked such an ugly flower. Such a small thing to feel relieved about. She fastened on the feeling for too long. She would have to open her eyes again. Wouldn't she?

Organ music swelled. Old, old gospel hymns, slave songs bade her grandson good-bye. She opened her eyes. Celeste was absent. She kept trying to die. They made sure she failed. Poor Celeste. Her child killed and the man she loved abandoned her all in the space of a moment. Would

Tiffany be able to leave her own pain long enough to do what she needed to do for her daughter-in-law? She hoped so.

What was that man saying? That minister had the presumption to pray to an uncaring God over her grandson's body. He was telling them that little Dante was alive somewhere with God. How did that man know? He'd never been dead, had he? That minister was simply parroting some words that had been spoon-fed to him. If God gave a damn about little Dante he'd be alive and happy right now.

Jenny pulled her to her feet and everybody was bowing their heads. Tiffany looked down at her feet. She hadn't seen Dante since she'd hugged him good-bye at Taylor's wedding. Tiffany's mind skittered. She would go and see Celeste after this service. She hoped she could do this one last thing to make things better if not right.

"I want to see Celeste. Please take me to her," Tiffany asked. Jason exchanged a worried glance with Jenny. He turned the car around.

The nurse had to unlock more than one door to let her in. Celeste was behind a heavy metal door with a small window of thick safety glass. The nurse unlocked the door and Tiffany entered. The room was the size of many walk-in closets Tiffany had had in her life. They had locked her up like an animal, Tiffany thought.

The walls were urine yellow cement block, the floor hard tile of puke green. What was to stop her from pounding her brains out against the wall? She looked up and saw the baleful eye of the video camera. Celeste was curled up on a single mattress that lay on the floor. She faced the wall. She wore scrubs whose color matched the floor, and her hair was uncombed, matted and dirty. She hadn't moved when the door had opened, people had entered the room, and the door had been locked behind them.

Tiffany sighed and went over and sat on a corner of the mattress. "Celeste," she said. "I wanted to talk to you."

Celeste didn't move. Only the rise and fall of her chest indicated she was alive.

"I was going to ask you to do something for little Dante. Then I realized that it didn't matter. Little Dante is dead. So I'm going to ask you to do something for me."

"Please go," Celeste said. Her voice was high, thin, like a child. She didn't sound like herself.

"No. I won't. But I have a slight idea how you feel. I've wanted to die most of my life. I decided not to around three years ago." Tiffany looked at her hands and took a deep breath.

"I didn't have good reasons like you do to want to die. My husband was alive and both my children were alive and healthy. I wanted to die because my husband didn't love me. Pretty stupid reason, huh?" She looked over at Celeste.

"I wanted to die because my life was miserable, but I had made it that way. Because my husband didn't love me, rather than either face the pain or change my life, I drank."

Celeste finally turned and stared at her. "I don't care about you. My husband is gone and my son is dead and I want to join him. He was who I lived for."

Tiffany nodded. "I understand more than you know. It makes sense, really. I thought you were a wonderful wife and mother. Ever since Dante married you, well . . . it seemed as if he glowed. I thought he'd learned to believe in himself and he became the man he could be. The last thing I said to him was that I was proud of him. Then I found out that he's . . . he's the worst part of me and his father. A drunk and a coward."

"Yes, he is." Celeste took a big, shuddery breath. "Why don't they leave me alone?" she whispered.

"Because it's their job not to. Because the ones who

care about you would feel terrible themselves if they did. It's all about them really."

"You're the first person to tell me the truth," Celeste said. "Everybody comes in here and tells me how much they care about me, or tells me my son is in a better place, or tells me that I don't know what the future holds and what God has in store for me." She gave a bitter laugh. "Somebody even told me that suicide is a sin. Why should I care if I sin against the God who let the worst thing I can imagine happen to me?"

"Why should God care?" Tiffany said. "He let my son live a lie and a baby die who never had a chance to live. The folks who pray for divine intervention are fools and full of vanity. Why would God do a damned thing for them when he allows the good and innocent to suffer, for heaven's sake?"

Celeste frowned at her. Tiffany smiled back, a cracked smile tinged with pain, but a smile nevertheless.

"I came here to ask you to go on despite the fact that it doesn't make a lot of sense right now," she said. "I'm not asking it because I care about you. I've always liked you, but I loved my son like a river. You couldn't stop it and it went on and on. The main thing I found good about you was that you made him happy."

"Why are you saying these terrible things to me? Now you know what Dante is," Celeste whispered.

"What Dante is doesn't change my love for him, it just makes it as painful as a razor. But you need to hear truth. I was going to ask you to live because you have your whole life ahead of you. But what does that matter? No, I want you to live for me. It's going to be hard enough for me to go on as it is. It's hard enough knowing what my son is, but it makes it so much harder knowing that his wife and the mother of my grandson is nothing but a weak, sniveling, coward."

Celeste gasped and her hand flew up. She slapped Tiffany across the cheek, hard.

"That hurt," Tiffany said.

"Get out!" Celeste screamed.

Tiffany shook her head at the people standing at the window ready to come in. "No, I'm not leaving yet. I'm not done."

"How dare you come in here and call me names?" Celeste yelled. "I lost my heart. I lost my baby. You monster! How dare you?"

Tears were running down her small face. "Get out, I beg of you, get out."

"No. I'm not done yet. What made me decide to live were my children. True, you don't have anything to live for anymore, but I haven't seen a shred of backbone in you, of courage, of determination. So this is what my son married. He got what he deserved."

Celeste shrieked in fury and launched herself at her. The door opened and the hospital staff burst in. Tiffany held Celeste, like Jason had held her through her own fury, shaking her head at the staff to stay back. Her will gave her strength to do this last thing she had to do for her son's wife.

Celeste calmed and great sobs racked her body as though they would rip her apart. Tiffany sunk to the floor with her, and rocked her like she was a baby while she cooed comforting mother noises at her.

The staff filed out of the room and a long while passed until Celeste's sobs subsided.

"Prove me wrong, Celeste. You have only one thing left to live for and that's yourself and your life. Prove me wrong about you, about God, about everything. Grieve the dead, but go on and live for yourself. That's what I want." She paused. "That's the only good thing that can come out of this tragedy."

Celeste raised her head and stared at her. "How was the funeral?"

"Terrible. Just terrible."

Celeste nodded. "Can you get me out of here?"

"No. They won't let you out until they know."

"I guess that's okay. There's not much demand on me in here. It's going to take me a while . . ."

Tiffany stood and smoothed her skirt. "I'm leaving now."

She knocked on the door and heard one of the nurses turn the key in the lock.

"Tiffany?" Celeste said.

She turned and looked back at her.

"Thanks."

Chapter 19

It was just a week after the accident and everyone assumed she'd packed up her grief and was going on with her life, Tiffany thought.

"Did you hear what I said?" Moira's voice sliced through her melancholy reverie.

"I'm sorry, could you repeat it?" she answered.

"I just said we're about ready to wrap up here. Are you okay?" Moira asked.

"I'm fine. Yes, it looks like I need to get cracking on the problem." The contributions had fallen off drastically since Verita left. It seemed as if she'd been bad-mouthing the organization and it was telling in their revenue.

The phone rang. "I'm going to take this call," Tiffany murmured. She picked up the phone.

"Mom?"

"Dante?" she whispered, gripping the phone so hard it hurt.

"I just came back. I'm in a lot of trouble . . ."

Anger seeped through her shock like molten lava. She looked into Moira's concerned face.

Moira touched her hand and exited the office, closing the door softly behind her.

"Mom, are you there?"

"I'm here. Yes, you're in a lot of trouble. Your son is gone and your wife is . . ."

"Celeste filed for divorce today."

"I don't blame her. You abandoned her and killed your son."

She heard a soft sound, something like a sob. "Why are you being so hard and cold? I've lost everything," he said.

"Why did you lie to me, Dante?"

"I never lied to you. I let you have your assumptions."

"You let me think you were a caring father and husband? A responsible person instead of somebody like your father—somebody who could kill his son and walk away."

"I'm not like my father. I'm like you. I'm a no-good drunk just like you were."

His words were like a punch in the stomach. She gasped and couldn't breathe.

"The truth too hard to deal with, Mom? You were all wrapped up in other people's children; you couldn't see what was happening to your own. Do you really think Jenny is that happy? Did she ever tell you what happened with that man she was seeing in Maryland?"

"No, no." Tiffany's words were a plea to him to stop.

"Why don't you ask her sometime? In the meantime, get up off your high horse of judgment and condemnation, look in the mirror and see yourself." He slammed the phone down in her ear.

Tiffany sat reading in her favorite spot on the front porch on the old-fashioned glider. Jenny came out through the screen door and said, "Mom, I'm looking into transferring to Washington University."

Tiffany put down her book and uncurled her feet from beneath her. "Oh? That would be wonderful." She looked into her daughter's beautiful face. She couldn't bring herself to ask the questions burning within her. *Are you happy, baby? What has happened in your life? Have I been there for you when you needed me?*

She was afraid to hear the answers.

"I like it in St. Louis," Jenny continued. "I need to make a change. I met this woman who desperately needs a short-term roommate until her lease is up. I think I'll stay with her and take my time finding a place of my own."

"Why not stay here?"

"Mom, get serious. This is your man's house. I can't stay here indefinitely. Besides, living with my mother is cramping my style."

Tiffany said nothing. She didn't tell Jenny that she needed her. She didn't mention that she felt like she was holding on by a thread. It didn't matter. Nothing she could say would make a difference. Jenny had made up her mind. She was going on with her own life.

"I'm going to go and start packing now. I'm planning to leave in the morning." Jenny smiled at her mother and left the porch without looking back.

Tiffany bowed her head and took a deep breath. She clenched her fingers into the palms of her hands until her nails dug into the skin. It hurt and that calmed her because it meant that she wasn't feeling the pain inside. She wasn't feeling the anger at Dante, the pain of losing her grandchild, and the disappointment that bordered on self-loathing because of her failures. For the moment she hung on. She picked her book back up.

* * *

The house was dark when Jason got in. It had only been a little more than a week since Jenny left, but it seemed as if the life and light had drained out of the house with her departure. Hungry, he headed for the kitchen. There was food on the stove. It was different from the food Tiffany used to cook, comfort food made from scratch and lovingly prepared. Now there was macaroni and cheese from a box, spaghetti with sauce from a jar, frozen prepared lasagna. But he was gratified that she was still making the effort. Not for him, but for herself.

He was growing increasingly worried about her. He held Tiffany against him every night until she slept, and he felt the pain emanate from her body in waves. He felt helpless in the face of it. He was a surgeon. He needed to fix things and make them all better. He didn't know where to begin. Tiffany had an open gaping wound where her heart used to be.

No, that was a poor simile. A wound, even an infected, foul wound with suppurating pus would be better than a broken heart. He knew how to approach that problem. He knew to clean out the infection and leave healthy pink and red tissue. If the patient was well-nourished and healthy, all he had to do was protect the wound and keep it clean. The body would heal itself. All it took was time.

But emotions were so much harder. He had no idea how to excise the pain so she could heal. He didn't know the source. She wasn't talking to him anymore. She'd drawn inside herself to some place he couldn't follow. He wished he could do more. She no longer wanted the sweet, wild sex they had discovered together. So he held her and she seemed grateful. He wished there was more he could do.

He fixed a plate as he heard the television in the den. Since her grandson's death and the revelations about her son, Tiffany spent hours sitting in front of the television. He barely saw her sit still for the evening news before, much less turn it on in the evening. The few free quiet evenings they had, they spent together. While he might be in front of a television for a game, she'd prefer to curl up on the couch next to him with a novel.

Now, after she got home from her job, she spent too many hours staring at vapid sitcoms or fast-paced, superficial dramas. She sat through talk shows and shows that featured some guy eating a bowl of worms and things of that sort. "Now I can see why they don't put black folks in their television shows," she'd said. "They feel they got plenty of us on *Jerry Springer* and *Cops.*" He'd grinned at her and took her hand, but the spark of life faded and she turned back to the television.

He took his plate and went in to her. She was sitting in front of the couch and he sat beside her. She didn't look up but stared at the moving figures on the television.

"Tiffany," he said.

She looked up at him with a slight frown. Irritation at being interrupted. It was so uncharacteristic of the woman he had known, his mouth dried and he momentarily forgot what he was going to say.

"I'm worried about you," he said instead. He set his plate down, no longer hungry, and got up to turn off the TV. She started to protest, but he saw her biting her lip. "It's been several weeks since . . . I'm seeing you slide into a depression."

"So you want me to see a shrink."

"I didn't say that, but yes, I think it would be a good idea if you saw somebody." He covered her hand with his. "I'm worried sick about you."

"I'm handling this, Jason. I don't need to see anyone. I've had my fill of mental health professionals."

"I disagree. I want to make an appointment for you. I know someone that I recommend."

"I told you I don't need to see a shrink! Why don't you leave me alone?"

"Because I care about you. You've changed."

She met his eyes fully then. "What do you mean?"

"You haven't budged from in front of this television for days. You're not taking care of yourself and you're not eating right."

She ran her hand over her hair. "I look a mess."

"That's not my point, baby. I'm worried about how you feel."

She kept talking like she didn't hear him. "We haven't made love . . . I haven't been keeping myself up."

"Those are the symptoms. I want you to see somebody."

"I don't need to see anybody. I just needed some time. I'm better now." She stood. "I'm going to take a bath."

She left the room. He stared after her and shook his head. He wanted to fix it for her so bad, it burned in his mouth. But she was right about one thing. What she needed was time. It was a certain healer.

Tiffany came to him that night. Sweet-scented and wrapped in expensive lingerie. She set him on fire. He made love to her with tenderness and passion. But . . .

Afterward, they always had the habit of lying together, neither wanting to pull free from the most intimate embrace. But tonight she curled into a ball as far away from him as she could get. He stared into the darkness. He hadn't reached her. He knew it was so. He'd gotten used to her responsiveness, to her wild passion. This was like making love to a shell.

He reached for her. "Tiffany," he said. "I'd like to talk." She moved away a little.

"I'm tired," she said.

She had to pull herself together. She had to pull herself together. It was a litany she repeated over and over to herself as she stared in her bathroom mirror and carefully applied her makeup.

When Jason said she'd changed, it shook her to the core. He was no longer finding her attractive. She had to pull herself together or she would lose him. Her hand slipped as she applied her lipstick and a red stain smeared against her cheek. She reached for a tissue with a shaking hand. Hell, she couldn't even put on makeup right. She'd have to reapply her foundation.

It was the kiss of death for a man to no longer find a woman attractive. First he'd stay away from home longer and longer. Then, before you knew it, the affairs would start. That's what happened with Sidney, and she understood it was a common pattern. She had a poor track record of holding on to a man. That was a fact.

He was becoming disgusted with her. At least with Sidney she'd had papers on him. This relationship was tenuous and based on the most fragile of bonds. What? Sex. Was that it? No, he liked her; he'd asked her to stay with him. He was unfailingly kind and gentle with her. He cared.

But he never said he loved her. He never said he wanted to spend the rest of their lives together. There was no commitment, no ties of love or at least loyalty. Did she measure up to the woman he still cried over thirty years after her death? Nope, no way was she the equal of her in his eyes. None of Diana's sons was a lying drunk who'd killed his own child.

Tiffany felt herself tremble. She squelched the emotion that she felt welling up from within her. She didn't want to feel a thing. Feelings pained her. Made her want to crawl in a pit and die. The only way she could go on was not to feel.

She knew that wasn't right for the majority of other people. When she first laid eyes on Celeste in the hospital, she knew that to bring the girl back to herself, she'd first have to get her feeling something. It was her mother's instinct that let her know she had to get Celeste mad enough to break open the doors to her emotion. She'd locked the pain down inside and she had to feel it before she could let it go.

This Tiffany knew, but she also knew her situation was different. She'd been wallowing in pain and dulling the edges with junk television. All it had gotten her was the disgust and disappointment of her man. She'd pull herself past her pain. She could do it. She had to.

"Are you sure you're okay?"

"I'm okay." Tiffany looked away, then met Moira's blue eyes. "I take that back. I'm not okay. I'm not okay with your assigning somebody else to this project."

Moira sighed. "The project is a key one. We have to raise more revenue or we're in deep trouble. What would you have me do? You obviously have been under great strain lately."

"I don't remember confiding in you," Tiffany said.

Moira's eyes narrowed. "No, you haven't."

Tiffany rubbed her hands over her eyes. "I'm sorry. I don't know what's come over me."

"That's all right. I can see something's wrong. If you do decide you need someone to talk to, I'm here."

"Thanks," Tiffany said. She wished she could confide in Moira, but the weight of her failures in life was too great to lay on anyone.

Moira stood up. "I have a meeting to get to. Janelle is simply your assistant. Her job duties are entirely under your discretion."

Tiffany stood also. She didn't know what else to say, so she simply nodded and returned to her office.

Where would she start? She knew what she should do. She should go down and hunt down that upstart Janelle and find out what she was doing. Take her job back. Instead she carefully propped her elbows on the desk and cradled her head in her hands. She had to pull herself together.

"Ms. Eastman?" Her head snapped up at Janelle's fresh young brown face.

"I'd prefer it if you knock before you enter my office."

"Of course." Janelle laid a sheaf of files on her desk. "I thought you'd like to see what I've done the past week."

Tiffany picked up a file, opened it and stared unseeingly at the black words on white paper.

"I'm willing to finish the Mosely grant if you're not up to it," Janelle continued. "Also the United Way pledge drive is getting into gear—"

"Thank you." Tiffany cut her off. This overeager, job-stealing child was getting on her nerves. "I'll let you know when I need you."

To her satisfaction Janelle seemed somewhat deflated.

"I'm always glad to help," Janelle said.

"I see."

Janelle shifted from one foot to another and turned to go. After the door shut behind her, Tiffany leaned back in her chair and shut her eyes.

Chapter 20

Jason's appetite had fled as he watched Tiffany pick at her dinner. An undercurrent of tension surrounded them, laden with unspoken words.

Tiffany broke the silence. "I want to talk to you," she said as Jason started to rise and carry his plate to the sink.

He sank back in his chair. "Good. Talking is good."

"There needs to be a change. Our relationship is bothering me."

A chill of fear ran through him.

"I want more, Jason."

A beat passed, two, before he realized that she was waiting for him to answer. "More of what?"

"More of you."

This was woman talk and it baffled him. It also left him uneasy. Was she telling him that he wasn't making her happy?

"I don't understand. What's wrong?" He wished there were more food on his plate to give his hands something to do. He stood and walked over to the stove and filled his plate again.

"You told me you wanted me to stay here with you in your house, but that's all you've said."

He sat heavily and tried to keep his face bland. He wanted to frown. "What do you want me to say?"

"I want a commitment."

He blinked and stared at the plate of food that suddenly had the texture and appeal of straw. His mouth was dry, but the ball was in his court and he had to say something. He picked up his water glass and took a long, slow swallow. "What sort of commitment?"

"Don't play dumb. Last time I noticed, you were fully grown. You know what I mean."

He felt attacked and defensive. He knew better than to say anything right now. So he carefully cut a piece of sawdust chicken, put it into his mouth and chewed it.

"Are you going to say anything to me?"

He swallowed. "I don't think it's a good time to discuss this . . ." He jumped from the sound of her open palm hitting the table.

"It's never a good time for you. I'm just someone to warm your bed and spread my legs whenever you feel like it. I'm just someone to keep you company. I want more and I'm worth more. I'm too old for this uncertainty, this wondering if I'm good enough. It's tearing me up inside."

"You want a commitment," he said, repeating her words back to her. It seemed the safest thing to do.

"Damn straight."

"Tiffany, you're under strain. It's not the time to discuss—"

"When is the time to discuss it? It's because of Diana isn't it? Your sainted wife is with us every minute of the day. She's in bed with us. She watches us every time you put your—"

"Enough! This conversation is over." He walked out of

the kitchen without looking back. He was so angry he didn't trust himself to speak.

Then he remembered the look on her face when she'd found out what Dante had done. The look of terrible pain and grief he'd only seen in the eyes of those who had lost the ones dearest to them forever. It takes time to recover from that sort of loss, and Tiffany hardly realized her pain. He turned and went back to the kitchen.

Her face was buried in her hands. He pulled up a chair next to her and pulled down her hands. "Listen to me. I care about you a great deal, and you're right, I do want you with me. I promise you this: we will talk about commitment. But the time is not right now. Our emotions are too raw and jagged. Do you understand?"

Her eyes were closed, her face turned away. He lifted her chin. "Do you understand how much I care about you?"

Finally, she nodded.

"I promise," he repeated. "Later."

Tiffany lay alone in her guestroom bed, washed in a sea of blue. Jason had wanted her with him. He wanted to make love to her, but she told him she needed to be alone, to think. She had not had a climax with him since little Dante died. Lovemaking had become what she previously had been accustomed to, not the transcendent experience it had been with Jason.

Intellectually she knew it was because of everything that had happened, but emotionally there was the nagging worry that he had finally discovered that she wasn't good enough. Like her late husband Sidney had discovered.

This morning she sat in her office and suddenly realized she was panting and drenched in sweat. She could do nothing but fan furiously with a manila folder. She remembered what her mother and aunts had gone through to recognize the symptom. It was her first hot flash. She had forgotten about that eventuality.

In her yearnings and the bloom of sexual discovery, she'd forgotten how old she was. Middle-aged. Her life was mostly behind her, and she had the withering of her womanhood to look forward to, just as she discovered it. She was scared and her emotions were a wild seesaw.

Now, Tiffany lay alone in her bed staring at the ceiling. She'd make an appointment with the doctor she decided. But what would he say? *You're getting old, Tiffany. It happens to the best of us.* And then she'd enter the world of hormone replacement therapy and ... menopause. She dreaded even thinking the word. Menopause, the death of femininity, of what made her a woman. She couldn't bear it.

She closed her eyes and willed sleep to come, but knew it was hours away. She got up and went to the bathroom. She drew open the medicine cabinet, looking for something, anything, to take the edge off, to help her to sleep and escape. There was a large bottle of Nyquil.

The popular cold medicine contained alcohol. But it was medicine and it was supposed to help you sleep. She took a double dose.

Tiffany pressed the print button and reached in the drawer for her purse. It had been a long, stressful day and she was glad it was over. She delivered the report to Moira's desk and let herself out of the empty office. Thank God it was Friday.

Because of the long summer days, she could catch the tail end of what must have been a wonderful day. Not too hot, plenty of cool breezes. Suddenly her life felt heavy and suffocating and she found herself turning into Houlihan's restaurant and bar. She'd have a bite to eat.

Moving toward the bar, she gazed at the tables and

booths that looked far too large for a woman alone. A woman alone and aging. A failure. The feeling crushed her like an avalanche. This was more than regret. This was anguish, topped off with a helping of self-hatred.

"Can I get you something?"

"Vodka martini. A double."

The words rolled off her tongue, unrehearsed and wholly unexpected. There was fear, but it was nothing compared to her need not to feel. The bartender nodded pleasantly and went to get her drink.

The liquor slid down her throat like melted ambrosia, nectar of the gods and just as magical. She felt the warmth of the alcohol spreading over her limbs and relaxing her body for the first time in weeks. The glass was empty much too soon.

"I'll have another," she said.

The second drink brought that pleasant, fuzzy blanket of numbness that she recognized well. What a comfort not to feel or to worry. The jagged edges were made smooth and soft. Warm as honey and just as sweet, she was. Yes, she was.

"Another," she said.

Later, she knew better than to drive. It was a rule. Three drinks, no drive. Or was it no drive, three drinks? Whatever. She asked the bartender to call her a taxi. She needed coffee. An Irish coffee would hit the spot while she waited. The butterfat in the cream would bind the whiskey alcohol molecules. Or so she'd heard somewhere. Everybody knew Irish coffee wouldn't make you . . . drunk.

"An Irish coffee please." The bartender hesitated, but she knew she was such a lady, so genteel; he wouldn't refuse her. One thing she could do was hold her liquor.

And so he didn't refuse her. My, it was good.

The taxi driver came in to get her after a while and she only stumbled once out to the car.

*   *   *

The house was lit up like a beacon. When the taxi pulled up, Jason rushed out the door. She gave the driver a twenty and got out of the taxi. So much for her quiet entry.

"I've been worried sick about you. The answering service at your office said you'd turned the phones over to them around seven. It's almost ten now. I couldn't imagine—" He stopped and looked after the retreating taxi. "Did you have an accident?"

"No. I just stopped and had a bite to eat. I took my time because I had some thinking to do. I'm very tired. I want to go to bed." She kept her face turned away from him and enunciated her words carefully. She walked around him and entered the house. She made it halfway to the bedroom when he grabbed her arm and turned her to him. "What's wrong with you?"

"I said I was tired. Please let me go."

He released her so suddenly she staggered and almost fell.

"You've been drinking," he said. The tone of condemnation mixed with horror in his voice was very clear.

She moved past him and went into her bedroom. The blue of the room burned her eyes. Or was it tears? She needed . . . to go to sleep. She dropped her clothes on the floor and went to take another dose of Nyquil.

Chapter 21

Jason stared at the television after Tiffany went into the bedroom. There was a knot in his stomach that was drawing tighter and tighter. When he couldn't locate Tiffany, it was as if one of his children was missing. But there was nothing for him to do but wait. It had been agonizing. The relief when he heard the car pull into the drive had been indescribable. He'd rushed to the door. His stomach had plummeted when he recognized the taxi, then he saw her get out. She was all right. It took only a few minutes and a few words from her to make him realize that she had been drinking. That she was drunk.

When he was a boy, he'd been waiting on his father to finish his haircut at the neighborhood barbershop. A woman had entered. She was loud and with tight, bright clothes and heavy makeup unlike he'd ever seen his mother wear. She laughed raucously and put her hands on the men. She smelled of strong perfume and alcohol. His father had paid the barber and rushed him away from the shop.

"That was a disgusting sight, son, and I have to apologize to you for letting you see it so young. That woman was a piece of trash. She's a drunkard and a loose woman. A woman like that is lower than the dirt on your shoes. Do you hear what I'm saying?"

He'd nodded solemnly.

"Your mother is the opposite of women like that woman in the shop," his father continued. "Women like your mother are clean and pure and they help you be a better man. Women like that woman in the barbershop make you dirty and low. You remember that, son. It's an important lesson."

He'd been impressed with his father's speech. He'd never forgotten. Diana, the first woman he dated, the woman he loved and married, was like his mother, sweet, gentle and good. Diana didn't drink or wear loud clothes or heavy makeup. Diana went to church every Sunday and had a deep and abiding faith in God.

But Tiffany ... last night she reminded him of that woman in the barbershop. When he tried to reason out how he felt about Tiffany, it was confused and tangled, and he'd soon given up. He could think of few things better than making love to her. So many things about her delighted him, her intelligence, her gentle ways, her maturity and her charm. He wanted her with him. It had gotten to the point where he couldn't imagine living in this house without her.

He'd let Tiffany into his home, into his bed. He'd asked her to stay with him. He'd been satisfied with her and thought she was satisfied with him. He'd given her far more than he'd ever given any woman before. She wanted more. She wanted commitment. She wanted vows and permanency. She wanted wedding bells.

But Tiffany transforming into a drunk was more than he could tolerate. What was he going to do? He couldn't live without her. He couldn't live with her drinking and her anger. She'd hit the ceiling when he'd suggested help. It was far more than he could handle. He didn't know what to do.

Tiffany rolled over, looked at the alarm clock and groaned. It was past nine. She had the thought that she would get up early and be out of the house before Jason stirred. Fat chance. The man was out of bed at six. She rolled out of bed and went into the bathroom. She turned on the shower and let the warm water rinse her clean and grant her absolution.

Tiffany pulled on a pair of jeans, a T-shirt, sneakers and a scarf over her head. She grabbed her purse and walked toward the front door, head down. She ran smack into Jason. He steadied her.

"We need to talk," he said.

"We don't have anything to talk about. I'll be out of here by the end of the day."

"Tiffany, don't go."

"I have to."

"You need help. Please. Do this for me."

"You think I'm weak, don't you?"

He didn't say anything, but she thought she could see the answer in his eyes.

"I'm stronger than you can imagine. Not out of choice, but out of necessity. I make your saint Diana look like the weak, spoiled woman she was."

His face froze. He didn't stop her as she walked out the door.

Tiffany stopped at one of those chain beauty shops. "I want to cut it off," she told the stylist.

"Would you like a swept-back style? Finger waves?"

"No. I want it all cut off. A short Afro, very close."

The stylist pursed her lips, but she got out her razor.

Afterward, she went to visit some apartment complexes. It was late afternoon when she realized she wasn't going to find a place to live today. It was the same scenario over and over. She'd call from the pay phone, peering at a display ad in the newspaper. They'd say there were vacancies and they'd be happy to show her some units. Then she'd arrive. Suddenly there would be talk about credit checks and reference verifications and waiting lists. The vacancies suddenly dried up and disappeared.

She pulled over by a corner liquor store on the way back to Jason's house. She bought a fifth of vodka and hid it under the seat. What did it matter if she drank or not? Everything she did turned to ashes. The comforting fuzzy blanket of alcohol made the pain of living endurable.

She walked straight to her bedroom, praying she wouldn't run into Jason. When she could get back out to the car and get the . . .

"Tiffany," Jason said.

She spun around. He stood there, silhouetted in the glare of the television from the den.

He took her in and his eyes widened. "What have you done to your hair?" he breathed.

"I cut it."

"That's obvious, but why?"

She shrugged.

He closed the space between them with a few steps. "My poor baby," he said, and he folded her in his arms. She couldn't yield to him. The pain inside her was too great.

"Please come in here," he said.

She let him lead her into the den, feeling apprehensive.

He took her hand. "I don't want you to leave. You need to stay here with me. We'll get through this."

She relaxed a little. Maybe . . .

"But I insist you get help," he continued. "The drinking cannot go on."

She withdrew her hand as her pain ignited a flare of anger within her. "How dare you give me an ultimatum?" she whispered.

"Look at you. It's not simply that you have fallen apart, it's that you refuse the help that's readily available."

"Look at me? Right. If I'm falling apart it's because I'm tired. Tired of everything. Tired of you."

Jason's eyes narrowed and he opened his mouth to speak.

"Don't say anything to me," she said. "I don't want to hear it. How you can help me is to leave me alone. As soon as an apartment comes through, I'm out of your life, do you understand? Then you can go back to bed with nothing but the memories of your dead wife like you are accustomed to doing."

She wheeled and walked away, slamming the door of her room shut behind her. Tiffany lay on her bed for an hour and stared at the blue ceiling. She had been truly awful to Jason, mean, spiteful and hateful. She pushed him away and gave up the game before it was over. Better to have a reason for the rejection he'd dole out to her. She imagined what he would tell her if she had tried to hold on to him. *It's not working out. Maybe we should see other people. I need some space.*

The pain built up inside her and she tried to endure it, to bear it, to let it pass on through her. It didn't, but it inched up to an unbearable pitch. When she wanted nothing more than to die, she gave up. She went out to the car and got the bottle.

Jason picked up the phone and punched in the numbers. Jenny picked up on the second ring. He cleared his throat. "This is Jason."

"Yes?"

"I'm calling to ask your advice on a problem."

"How can I help you?"

He hesitated, his fingers clenching the receiver. He knew of no way to put it delicately. "Your mother is drinking."

Jenny gasped. "Are you sure?"

"She came home in a taxi last night. Her speech was slurred and she reeked of alcohol."

"Oh, God."

"She went looking for an apartment today. I begged her to get help, but she refused. She's changed. Every time I try to talk to her she gets angry. And she cut off all her hair, Jenny. She's virtually bald."

"Where is she now?"

"She's in her room."

"You have no idea how serious this is. My mother is a strong woman. There is no way to describe the hell my father put her through. She's been abstinent from liquor for three years."

"She's been depressed since before you left. I tried to get her to get help, but she refused."

Jenny was silent for a moment. "I'll be right over," she said.

Jason replaced the receiver back in its cradle carefully. He hoped he had done the right thing in calling Jenny. He prayed that Tiffany would be all right, but he couldn't deal with this. He'd try to talk to Tiffany one more time and tell her Jenny was coming.

Jason knocked on the door to her room. There was no answer. He knocked again. Alarmed, he tried the door. It was locked. "Tiffany," he called. "Tiffany, are you all right?"

Nothing. He put his shoulder to the door and a moment later burst into the room.

"Get . . . get out," she said.

She sat in the middle of her bed, a fifth of liquor cradled in her lap.

"My God," he said.

She slid off the bed and set the fifth carefully on the dresser. "I could use some orange juice," she said, and moved past him.

"You are not drinking under my roof."

"I'll be out from under your roof shortly, so I fail to see how making an allowance for a day or two would be a problem for you."

She started out the door, but stopped and retrieved the bottle. "It was getting stuffy in the bedroom anyway," she said. She walked toward the kitchen.

He followed, feeling at a loss. "Are you drunk?" he asked.

"Yep, and getting drunker." She peered into the refrigerator and got out a carton of orange juice. Taking a tumbler off the shelf, she filled it with vodka and topped it off with juice.

"You aren't drinking that. Stop this drinking right this instant!" Jason roared.

Tiffany calmly screwed the cap back on the bottle. "I guess I need to inform you that you are not my father, my minister, the police or my boss. And the last time I checked I was over twenty-one and fully grown."

"I am the owner of this house and I deserve respect." He grabbed the glass of vodka and orange juice and poured it into the sink.

Tiffany's eyes narrowed.

He moved toward the bottle and she snatched it off the table. "You've crossed the line now, you son of a bitch," she screamed. "It's on."

He stopped short and stared at her.

"Touch this bottle and I'll carve your goddamn heart out," she yelled.

He held up his hands and backed away. "You won't need to bother. You aren't worth the trouble. You disgust me." He wheeled and left the room, grabbed the keys and headed for his car. If she wouldn't leave, he sure as hell could.

The door slammed so hard behind him, the house shook.

When Jason slammed the door it reverberated on and on within Tiffany, vibrating her bones and turning her heart to jelly. She'd seen the disgust and rejection in his eyes. It was done. They were done. The man she loved had looked at her as if she were a bad odor.

She slid down the refrigerator and sank to the floor. There was no room left inside her for any more grief. She was a hole, a space of black nothingness that didn't matter. She unscrewed the top off the vodka and took a large swallow. It burned her throat and she coughed, wiping her mouth with her T-shirt.

A few years ago, she chose to live for her children. They needed her. But now what did she have? She had failed with her children. They were both unhappy, the true legacy of her and Sidney. She'd tried so hard. Her kids were everything to her. But she'd failed. She whimpered. She took another swallow of vodka, smaller this time.

Tiffany struggled to her feet. She took the bottle and the carton of orange juice to her room and set them carefully on the bedside table. She pulled back the covers and got into the bed fully dressed. Hefting the carton of juice, she debated whether she should pour the juice into the vodka bottle or the vodka into the juice carton? It was the most momentous decision in her world right now. She decided on the latter and carefully emptied the vodka into the carton.

She lay back against the headboard. Yes, this was her world. It was regrettable the trouble dealing with her would cause Jason, but she didn't doubt that he'd have her shipped somewhere if she wasn't ambulatory. She didn't feel like ever walking again. She took a swallow of the vodka-fortified orange juice. Much better. She sighed as the fuzzy warmness descended to cover her and blanket her cares and grief as she wandered lost through the endless empty vista.

Jenny rang the doorbell another time. No answer. She pounded on the door. "Mom?" she called. "Jason?" He'd called her less than forty-five minutes ago. Where were they?

Jenny walked around the house. There was no sign of life, the windows all were tightly closed. A slight twinge of alarm touched her.

She needed to get into the house, at least to be able to check the garage and see if their cars were there. She went to the porch and got what looked like a sturdy chair. Praying that the neighbors didn't take it into their heads to call the police, she started trying the windows.

The third one she tried slid open. She stood on the chair and struggled to heave herself up. She fell through the blinds, crashing to the floor along with them. She struggled to her feet, entangled in the string and aluminum. Nobody must be home because, with the racket she just made, if they were they'd have come running with baseball bats in hand.

It was Jason's bedroom and she'd made a mess of his window treatments. Good thing he was so easygoing. It took a while to extricate herself.

She went to the garage. Jason's car was gone, but her mother's Camry was there. That meant they either went somewhere together or her mother was . . . She moved to the bedroom her mother was staying in. The door was slightly ajar.

Chapter 22

Jason went to the hospital after the fight with Tiffany. His anger soon faded and only a lost, desolate feeling remained. What the hell was he going to do? No answer. He did another entirely unnecessary set of rounds, needlessly upsetting the residents. He got a call room and stared at CNN for a couple of hours. Larry King was moderately entertaining, but the news was enough to drive a sad person to suicide.

He had told the service to forward his calls to him instead of the surgeon on call. He checked his beeper to see if it was working. His beeper was fine.

He turned off the television and lay back on the uncomfortable hospital bed. He wanted to go to Tiffany; he wanted to talk about it with her through the night. He wanted to make it all better, but she wasn't in her right mind. She was drunk and probably getting drunker. This drama in his life wasn't welcome. He couldn't go on like this. Why was she so bent on destroying what they had together?

After tossing and turning for a while, he got up. He was going home. Running away from a problem was not a man's way. No, he'd have to face it. On the way out of the room the realization hit him that it was the first time in his life that he'd craved a drink.

Jenny entered the room and swallowed hard. Her mother was sprawled across the bed dressed in jeans and a T-shirt and what looked like a very close-cut fade. A light snore emanated from her throat. A fifth of vodka was on the bedside table and an empty carton of orange juice on the bed.

Jenny's head dropped and her eyes moistened. She should have never left her. She approached the bed and sat on the edge. Alcohol emanated from her mother's pores. She shook her shoulder gently. Tiffany groaned and pulled away. "Mom, wake up."

She shook her with more force. Tiffany's eyes flew open and focused on the ceiling with some difficulty.

"Damn," Tiffany said.

Jenny nodded. Her mother's word had been loaded with moaning and emotion.

"Jenny," Tiffany croaked. Then she rolled off the bed and stumbled into the bathroom. Jenny heard her mother being sick. Then the shower came on.

A few minutes later, Tiffany emerged with a towel wrapped around her. She stumbled to her chest of drawers and pulled out a pair of panties, jeans and a T-shirt.

"Where's Jason?" Tiffany asked.

Jenny heard the slur in her words. "He's not here."

"It figures, that no-good dog. The measure of a man is when the going gets tough. That's when they lift up their tails and book."

"Mom, you're drunk. Why don't you lie down and we'll talk in the morning. I'll stay the night."

"If you think I'm lying down in one of Jason Cate's beds again, you're kidding. I'm getting out of here. I can't get an apartment, so I'll get a hotel." She opened her closet and started yanking out suitcases. "Help me pack."

"Mom, you should reconsider. Jason cares for you deeply."

"Years of my life down the drain because of a man. It's always a man. Honey, don't let one of them destroy you. I lost my best years because of Sidney Eastman. I'm not losing the rest on Jason Cates." She threw a suitcase on the bed and emptied the contents of a drawer into it.

"That's not a fair comparison. Please calm down. You're putting all that happened in the past with Dad and all that's happened with Dante on Jason. You know that's not fair."

"Who the hell said anything about life was fair?" Tiffany stopped ripping clothes from hangers, and her head dropped. "I can't get back on my feet with Jason. I'm too scared. Please help me get out of here."

Jenny nodded. She knew where her mother was coming from. Mom was scared of Jason's rejection, so she had to leave first.

Jason let himself into his home. Tiffany's car was gone and every instinct he had told him something was wrong. He went straight toward Tiffany's bedroom. The room was spotless, the bed neatly made. He threw open the closet door. The closet was empty. She was gone.

He couldn't believe it. The fact rattled and rolled within him. The house echoed with emptiness. He had to find her. What if . . . He couldn't finish the thought. Did Jenny ever come? What if Tiffany were alone? What if Tiffany were drunk . . . what if she were drunk somewhere? What if she were driving? What if she were alone? He picked up the phone and dialed Jenny's number. The answering machine clicked on and he hung up.

With increasing panic, he wondered who else he could call on a Sunday night to locate her. Maybe her stepdaughter Kara would have an idea. He forced his hand to relax on the receiver while the phone rang two, three times. "Hello?"

"Kara, this is Jason Cates."

"Hello, Jason. What can I do for you?"

"Tell me, have you heard from Tiffany or Jenny? I'm trying to locate either one of them."

There was a pause on the other end. Jason felt a bead of sweat trickle down his temple. "Do you know where they are?"

"Jenny said she was taking Tiffany to a hotel."

"Which one?"

"She said she'd call as soon as she got her mother settled in."

"Do you know which hotel?"

"No. When they left your house, I don't think they knew either. Have you tried Jenny's apartment?"

"She's not in." With a feeling of despair, he gave Kara his beeper number and told her to call as soon as she heard anything.

How could Tiffany leave him without a note or a word? He'd opened his home to her. He'd opened his life to her, his heart—He stopped and sank on the sofa. He thought he could deal with almost anything, but the shock of seeing her drunk and the foul curses that poured from her mouth were too much. He simply couldn't deal with it and he'd walked out on her.

But somewhere inside, he knew that wasn't Tiffany, but the pain and depression and stress coming out. The shadow side of the human psyche. Everyone had one.

If Tiffany was willing to try and conquer her dark side, he was willing to walk beside her. He couldn't bear it alone in this house without Tiffany. Without love and laughter, it was nothing but a mausoleum and a shrine to long-gone memories. He lay down on his bed and closed his eyes. Sleep would take him beyond his pain.

"You had a slip, Mom. That's not the important thing," Jenny said.

Tiffany squinted against the morning light. She felt like road kill. At the moment her main regret was that she was still breathing. "It's not? What's the important thing?" she managed to say to her daughter.

Jenny took a few steps to her mother and embraced her. "The important thing is that we have each other and we're here for each other. I need you, Mom. You're all I have."

Warmth and love overcame Tiffany's discomfort. She gave Jenny a wry smile. "I more than slipped, honey. I fell flat on my butt."

"I'm here to help you back up right now. There's absolutely no reason for you to stay down on the floor. Take my hand and step up."

The pain yawned in front of Tiffany, a deep gulf she didn't think she could bridge. She shook her head. "I can't," she whispered.

"When you found out about Dante's troubles, you believed everything good you'd accomplished in your life was gone, right? I always suspected that he was your favorite, but I had no idea I meant so little to you."

Tiffany flinched. "You know what you mean to me."

"No. No I don't know. I need you, Mom, but not as some drunk I'm continually going to have to rescue. I need my mom. Dante needs you too, now more than ever."

Tiffany closed her eyes. "When Dante called me, I was cold and unfeeling, lost in my own pain. I told Celeste she was a weak, sniveling coward because she refused to face the pain and get through it."

Tiffany gazed at Jenny. "I told my boss a while back that the strong black woman was dead," she said. "I guess I lied. I'm still alive and kicking. I'll go on. I always have."

"I don't know too many women who can measure up to you. Things got to you and you drank, but you were still always there for us. And you've always been there to help others. Celeste was only the last one who needed you. There have been lots before and there will be a lot from now on. Please don't give up, Mom."

"No, I won't give up." Her gaze sharpened and focused on Jenny. "I lost Jason. The first man in my entire life who I could lean on . . ."

"I doubt if he'll allow himself to stay lost. He called me last night. He cares about you, but this is something that I doubt that he's had to deal with personally before."

"When things got rough, he left."

"I think in your state last night you were too much for him to handle."

Tiffany closed her eyes. She couldn't face the loss of Jason at this moment. "Jen, could you go and get me some Tylenol?"

It was Sunday morning and Jason got dressed to go to church. He got in his car and as he approached the church, he imagined Tiffany's incredibly beautiful voice swooping and sailing around his heart. Jason drove on past the church. He couldn't go in without her at his side.

He soon found himself at the cemetery where Diana was buried. He got out of the car. The slam of the door echoed through the still of the place. It was an old cemetery. Ancient trees still stood guard.

She was buried near a willow tree. The sky was clear and almost neon blue with the approaching twilight. The air was fragrant with newly mown grass, and yellow butterflies flitted through the air. He fell to his knees by her grave and pushed his fingers under the grass into the cool, black earth.

"I wonder what you would have looked like now?" he whispered. "Thirty years. You never knew your daughter, Taylor. She just got married to a fine man. Stone Emerson is his name."

He sat back on his knees and clasped his hands, bringing them to his lips. "Tiffany loved her wedding. In many ways she's tried to stand in for you with Taylor. I've never told you about Tiffany, have I? But she's gone now. She left me. She had a drinking problem. No, that's not quite right. In the past, she had a drinking problem. Things just got to be too much for her and . . ."

He pulled at the stalks of grass. "We didn't talk enough about things, I guess. We had a lot of sex."

He bit his lip. "I'm sorry." He shifted and sat for a while, staring into the distance.

"I think I've made some mistakes. I can't—I can't go back to that house and be alone anymore. When I was with her, I felt whole. I never wanted her to leave. But when she pressed for a commitment, I panicked. What if she never licks this problem with alcohol?"

The wind blew through the willow, rustling the leaves.

"She told me once that it wasn't a moral failing, it was a disease that she controlled. I can't see her not getting things back under control. She's competent and strong, yet all woman." He dropped his head. "If I hadn't been so afraid to give her my all, she might not have fallen."

The wind whistled as if it agreed.

"I didn't look in my heart. I can't do without her, Diana. Do you understand? Is it right for me to move on without you?"

The leaves rustled. The breeze caressed his face and he felt at peace.

"Good-bye, Diana."

He stood and walked back to his car. He didn't look back.

Tiffany and Jenny were ensconced in a hotel room and waiting for a pizza to arrive. Koko Taylor's voice boomed out of a portable CD player as she belted out the blues. *I got what it takes to make a bulldog break his chain.*

"God, I want a drink," Tiffany said.

"Three days, and it'll get better. The edge of the craving will dissipate." Jenny studied her mother. "You should go into treatment."

"Maybe I should, but I don't think I need that. I just need myself."

"I don't understand."

"I'd lost myself before Dante had his accident, lost myself in a man. You were right to be concerned when you first came to St. Louis. I wasn't taking care of myself."

"Because you'd stopped going to meetings and paying attention to your abstinence?"

"More than that. I was all wrapped up in being physically carried away by a man. All I cared about was pleasing him. What he thought about me. Not making waves. Not bringing up the bothersome subjects. Anything to keep him happy and turned on. It wasn't Jason's fault, though. It was me."

Jenny rolled over on her stomach and propped her head on her hand. "I know exactly what you mean."

"You do?"

"Sure. I think most women do. That is, if they are lucky to have their minds blown by a gooood man."

Tiffany laughed out loud.

"Seriously, Mom, I have to know. Why did you cut your hair off like that?"

Tiffany touched her head. "It looks really bad, huh?"

"Not really. It's just so different from what I'm used to. You have a nicely shaped head."

"You know why I did it? I wanted a new me, a rebirth. I'd been thinking of cutting it for a while. I was sick of the relaxed hair thing. The chemicals, the curling irons, the endless upkeep of fighting my hair to force it to assume a texture totally unnatural to it. I couldn't imagine braids or locks suiting me."

"Believe me, they wouldn't."

"One option was to cut it short and wear a neat Afro. Ah, the freedom. Although it took me getting drunk to actually do it."

Jenny chuckled. "I bet Jason about had a heart attack when he saw you."

"Ohhhhh, you should have seen his face." Tiffany's face suddenly crumpled. "My God, I've screwed up. It seems as if I've lost everything important to me except you."

"You haven't lost the things that matter most," Jenny said. "Yourself and anyone who truly loves you. That's all that really matters in life."

Chapter 23

Tiffany called into the office Monday morning without a qualm of guilt and said she wouldn't be in. Then she made an appointment to meet with a highly recommended therapist experienced in addictions. Shopping, reading, long bubble baths and experimentation with the makeup to go with her new hairstyle took up the rest of her time.

Every time a thought of Jason came to her mind, which was often, she forced it away. She needed this time to regain her equilibrium, and she couldn't do it dealing with him. He'd left messages at the hotel switchboard. She knew Jenny called and told him she was okay. For today that was enough. She still had herself, she reminded herself. She'd face the thought of life without Jason tomorrow.

Dusk fell as Tiffany and Jenny strolled through the neighborhood of Central West End. Tiffany stopped abruptly as she spied a lovely Victorian mansion with a "For Rent" sign in the front. "Look at that house." Tiffany drew in a breath. It was perfect. It looked like a brick gingerbread cottage, albeit a large one. Turrets and flourishes with some of the most beautiful brickwork she'd ever seen. The windows were leaded glass jewels. The house was full of soul and mood and beauty, everything she needed. "I'm going to knock on the door," she said.

Jenny trailed her. A tiny, elderly white woman opened the door. "Can I help you?"

"I saw the 'For Rent' sign."

"Yes, we have a two-bedroom apartment. It's up a flight of stairs. Travis!"

Tiffany flinched and Jenny started from the woman's sudden shriek. It was even more alarming when a Viking appeared.

That's what he looked like, Tiffany thought. The man had to be almost six and a half feet tall. He had long blond hair that most white women would have happily killed him for and piercing blue eyes. Overall, he was very alarming looking. Then Tiffany noticed Jenny. Her brown eyes had turned into saucers and he was cow-eyeing her right back. Her little Jenny with a Viking a foot taller than she? Nah.

"You're interested in an apartment?" he asked Jenny.

"Yes, I am," Tiffany replied.

He turned to her, seeing her for the first time. "I'll show it to you. Grandma, I'm going to take them on up," he repeated to the old lady loudly.

"Boy, I can hear. Get on."

"Her deafness appears to come and go," he whispered to Jenny.

"Don't talk about me like I'm not here. I'll tan your hide," the gentle, delicate-looking old lady yelled at the huge Viking.

"All right, Grandma."

He motioned for them to follow and they walked out the door to a stairway that ran up the side of the house. "There's a separate entrance. The door to the main house has been blocked off." He opened the door and let them in.

Tiffany gasped. High ceilings with tall windows framed by some of the most intricate and beautiful woodwork she'd ever seen flooded the room with buttery light filtered through gauzy curtains. The floors were highly polished wood, and a huge fireplace with ornate woodcarvings that matched the woodwork graced the room.

"I'll take it," Tiffany whispered.

"Ma'am? You haven't seen the rest of the apartment."

"It doesn't matter."

It only took an hour to finish up the formalities and Tiffany signed a check with a flourish.

She looked up to say something to the Viking, or Travis as he was called, and saw him bent over her daughter. They were both laughing at something.

"I'll pick you up at seven," Travis said.

Tiffany's eyebrows shot up. Jenny had accepted a date with the Viking. My, my.

She handed the check over, and they were back in the sunshine within minutes.

"I can't believe that you rented that place so quickly," Jenny said. "My therapist said that impulsive decisions—"

"Are sometimes right when you're following your intuition and your heart. What I can't believe is that you're going out with that guy. When did your taste change from the Jared type?"

Jenny looked a touch bemused. "I don't particularly know what my tastes are."

"Hmmmm, I'd say not. That house was gorgeous. The brickwork alone would cost a fortune today. Did you see the stained glass windows? And that wood molding. I'd love to have that entire house one day."

"Who knows? Maybe one day you can buy it. Travis told

me that they wished his grandmother would move into somewhere she could manage more easily."

Jenny had left on her date, and Tiffany curled up on the hotel bed with an order of giant shrimp, strawberries and sparkling white grape juice. Ambrosia. She picked up one newly released video, then another, wondering which one she'd watch first.

She was ready to reclaim her life. The inner guide that she'd lost was back. The pain and grief at the loss of her grandson and the image she'd held of her son were still there, but now she had the faith in herself that she wouldn't allow negativity to overwhelm her. She mattered. Thank you, God, she still mattered. She didn't know what hour it was that she found her faith again. But from one instant to the next, what she thought was lost was fully restored.

Was it the sight of her daughter's sleeping face that did it? Jenny had fallen asleep in front of the TV. Tiffany watched her and remembered. Remembered the joy she had taken in both her children, remembered how despite all her own problems, she'd always put them first.

She could look back on her life and say, *with God's help I was the best mother I knew how to be regardless of how my children turned out.* The home she and Sidney had made together was dysfunctional because of the collision of her weaknesses with his mad selfishness. But her weaknesses never included a lack of love for her children, only for herself. Her love for them was the river that ran through her, the anchor that always brought her back to reality.

Tiffany found herself and her faith again, but she was still struggling to conquer her fear. She'd been afraid of Jason and the pain that his rejection could cause her. Her fear would disrupt the delicate balance she was trying to seek and send her tumbling into despair . . . and alcohol. Fear existed within her, but intellectually she knew it made no sense. Although lives end and change forever in an instant, what mattered most was one's moment in time. Not the past, not the future, but right now. It was all simply a lesson and an experience in the circle of life. There was nothing to fear. Nothing ended the cycle. Everything returned to the source and went back out again.

Even so, she grieved that the cycle of her life would no longer include Jason.

Tiffany had finished up her report to Moira about the success of the last fund-raising project and leaned back in the chair next to Moira's desk, waiting for her reaction to it.

"I love your hair," Moira suddenly said.

Tiffany touched her head, pleased. "Thanks."

"You look a lot better. I was worried about you."

"My grandson's death and the events surrounding it were very hard for me to deal with. But I do feel better now."

Moira nodded. "You take care of yourself," she said.

"I will. I'm the most important thing I've got." The secretary buzzed and Moira picked up the phone, listened and set it back on the cradle. "You'll want to get back to your office. There's a Jason Cates waiting there to see you. Oh, by the way, your report was great."

Jason. Tiffany's mouth dried. She'd missed him so much. She wasn't ready to face him. But she squared her shoulders and strode to the reception area.

He raised his head at her approach, and he looked so fine, she caught her breath.

"Hello, Jason," she said.

He stood and wiped his hands on his pant legs. "Can we talk?" he asked.

"My office is this way."

He looked around her office, his eyes lingering on the Brenda Joy Smith prints on the walls. "Nice place."

"Yes, WomenHelp is a wonderful agency. We administer

a variety of programs designed to help women gain and maintain independence."

"Admirable. But I know what the agency does. I came here to talk about us."

She bit her lip. "Would you like something to drink? Some coffee maybe?"

"No."

"I need some. I'll be right back." She took her coffee mug and fled. In the break room, she poured her coffee and reached for the half-and-half, pouring it in slowly and watching the white swirl together with the brown coffee into an entirely new color. She must not let whatever Jason said draw her off course. She had to take care of herself. That did not include losing herself in a relationship that didn't give her all she needed.

What did she need? It was simple actually. She needed security in love. Commitment, someone to grow old with. It was a lot more than sex, more than compatibility, more than affection. But was she merely accommodating her fear? Was security worth more, was fear worth more than love? She swallowed hard.

She'd been gone a moment too long. He leaned forward in his chair, his elbows on his knees, his head drooped. He looked bereft and vulnerable. There was nothing she wanted to do more in that moment but snuggle into his broad chest and be wrapped in his loving arms.

She started to sit behind her desk but changed her mind and sat at the little round table. He got up and sat across from her.

"How are you?" he asked.

She knew very well that his question wasn't a casual one.

"I'm fine." Neither was her answer.

"Good. I'm glad." He looked at his hands. "I want to apologize."

"I'm the one who needs to apologize, Jason. You know

that. I was the one who got drunk under your roof, who cussed you out, who—"

"You'd had all you could take. I should have . . ." He sighed. "I should have stayed."

"You did what you could."

"Are you sure you're okay?"

A tinge of anger drew a finger over the raw nerves of her emotion. "I said I was fine. What you want to know is if I'm drinking, is that right? The answer is no. I had a slip and now it's over."

"Good. I'm pleased."

"Not nearly as much as I." Tiffany set her cup carefully on the table. "Is that all you have to say to me? If so, I need to get back to work."

"No, that's not all I have to say to you. I came here to ask you to come back home with me."

Tiffany looked away from him. "I just got a new apartment," she said. "I'm really excited about it."

He reached out and took her hand. "Tiffany, please."

She withdrew her fingers from his. She wouldn't settle. Not with a man she loved as desperately as she loved Jason Cates. It would break her.

It was unlikely that at her age she'd ever get the commitment and security she craved. But she had her family and friends. She would make a life and when she died she'd know that she mattered in the ways that count. Most of all, she had herself.

"No. I'm not going back to your house," Tiffany said. "You want company and sex, and those two things shouldn't be hard for a man like you to find."

He looked as if she'd hit him. "That's not true. I need . . . I need for you to come back home."

"It's not my home. You know that. It will never be my home. You know who that house belongs to." She stood and walked to the window and stared out. She was crying inside, but she had to be firm. "The problem is that we both have issues that we never faced alone, much less together." When I'm with you, the craving, the yearning, overtakes everything. I lost myself," she said, turning to face him.

He opened his mouth and she raised her hand. "Please, let me finish. I can't go back with you right now. Not until I'm stronger." She turned and faced the window again.

Silence fell for almost a full minute and she waited with steely self-discipline to hear the sound of the door shutting behind Jason.

Instead she felt a touch on her back and his soft voice in her ear. "I wish we could start all over."

She closed her eyes but didn't move.

"We took off like a rocket," he said from close behind her. "We'd barely been together twenty-four hours before we made love. Our passions carried us away as though we were teenagers again. We didn't take the time to get to know one another intimately before we joined our lives together. We didn't talk enough. We never faced our fears or worked through our issues like we should have done—together."

He took a shuddery breath. "If I had one wish, it would be to start over at the beginning and do it right. I'd ask for another chance for us not to throw away what we could have together."

His voice was like a caress. "I'd take you out on a date Saturday night and leave you at your door with only a good night kiss. I'd talk to you for hours over Sunday brunch in an outdoor café. I'd take you for picnics in the park. I'd be your date, and then I'd be your best friend. I'd learn your darkest secrets, your deepest intimacies and your biggest fear, and you'd learn mine. And then, and only then, I'd be your lover."

Tiffany exhaled. She slowly turned to meet his eyes, the yearning in her heart bursting to overflowing. But she heard the office door close softly behind him. He was gone.

Chapter 24

"How about going fishing tomorrow?" Jason asked.

"Sounds good. But as I glance over to my caller ID I see you're calling from St. Louis. Atlanta is quite a drive for a casual fishing date tomorrow," Marvin Reynolds answered.

Jason moved the phone to a different ear. "I'm taking off a few days. I'm moving."

"What! You mean you're finally shifting your old tired body from that mausoleum you call a house? Does this mean wedding bells are ringing?"

"Tiffany left me."

"Oh. I'm sorry. I could tell she meant a lot to you. I was hoping . . ."

"So was I."

There was a silence between them, the silence between men that spoke volumes.

"I put the house on the market," Jason finally said.

"Sounds like you finally got some sense. Moving on after

thirty years in that house. You've been stuck in a serious rut."

"I know. Things are going to change now, though. I can't let her go. She asked me to stay away, but I'm going to think of something."

Marvin cleared his throat. "What time are you thinking about going fishing? Ain't a whole lot of point unless you go early."

"I'm taking the red-eye flight. I'll be at your front door at five in the morning."

"All right. That sounds good."

Jason hung up. He was desperate to get away from this house, to reevaluate things in a different surrounding. Seeing his old friend and doing some fishing was what he needed. Marvin might be direct to the point of bordering on rudeness, but he wasn't insensitive. He must have discerned Jason's need, thus didn't question the wisdom of traveling hundreds of miles for a fishing trip.

Jason felt like he'd lost his heart, his soul. He knew Tiffany needed time, but it was difficult to be patient. He needed her so badly.

Jason stuck his fishing rod into the holder on the side of the boat. He popped open a beer. "Lake Lanier gets better every time I come."

The waves lapped against the boat and the early morning air still had a chill to it.

"Yes. It's nice out here. It's been a while since I've been out fishing. So when are you going to tell me what's going on with you and that woman? She impressed Edna, and that takes some doing. That's obviously why you flew all the way out here."

"It blew up in my face. I'm still reeling from the aftershocks."

"Want to talk about it?"

"Not really."

Marvin nodded and they watched the water for a while.

"I'm getting offers for the house already," Jason said.

"I'm not surprised. It's a great house. But I've wanted to tell you to sell that house for the past ten years. I can understand how you wanted to raise your children there, but old ghosts were keeping you from moving on. I was worried about you."

"Why didn't you say something? You were never the type to bite your tongue."

"Hell, man, every time I started to bring up the subject, you'd act like I was getting ready to talk you into shooting your dog."

"I wasn't ready."

"No, you weren't."

"That's one reason why I lost her. I've been a bachelor for thirty years, haunted by the ghost of my wife. In my mind, no woman ever measured up to her. Until I met Tiffany."

"What's the other reason?"

"What?"

"The other reason why you lost her."

Jason sighed. "Those old ghosts. She had them too, and we never exorcised them together. We rarely talked about the things that mattered."

"Why not?"

"We were making too much love."

Marvin chuckled. "That's a good reason." He took a swig of his beer. "The woman loves you. I saw it in her eyes. Do I get to be best man or are you giving it to one of your sons?"

"She told me she wanted me out of her life, and you're talking about wedding plans?"

"You worry too much, Jason. I can see that you're not letting her go. I know you well enough to know that once you make up your mind you're going to have something, you're as persistent as a hound worrying a bone."

"I suppose so, but I'm not nearly as optimistic as you. But tell you what, if it's true, you definitely get to be best man."

"Damn. I hate weddings."

"Yours was pretty good."

"My own doesn't count."

"How's married life treating you this time around?"

"A damn sight better than the last time. Thank God my ex-wife got a job out of town. She was hanging around so much I knew my wife Edna and her were going to scrap. If that happened I was going to get out of the vicinity rather than get between them, since I have no desire to end up in the hospital."

"You wouldn't protect your new wife?"

Marvin guffawed. "Protect Edna? The only protecting to be done would be of my ex, Donna. If Edna raised a hand to her, the kindest thing I could do for my ex-wife would be to call 9-1-1 so at least she'd get medical treatment quicker."

"You're a mess, Marvin. But really, was marriage worth it?"

Marvin's face sobered. "It was worth all that and more. If you have a chance to have the love of a good woman, hold on to it. There's nothing worse for a man than to grow old alone. Not many men will admit this, but we need them more than they need us."

"I know," Jason said, staring into his beer at the disappearing bubbles of foam. Every moment without her was as lost as one of those bubbles. If only she needed him as much as he needed her.

Tiffany filled her new home with simple furniture and splurged on small objects of beauty that caught her eye.

A delicate cut crystal vase filled with fresh blooms, a small painting by an obscure African artist that she wanted to stop and study every time she passed. An antique clock, a single white calla lily. All of it only helped a little to lighten her heart, and none to ease her loneliness.

She kept busy. She filled her days with activities to ward off the empty hours at home that gave rise to temptation. The seductive alcoholic blanket of not caring and blessed near oblivion was always only a drink away. She chose to live her life instead. Such as it was.

A day went by, then another and another, and Jason still hadn't called. How many times had she picked up the phone and stared at it, aching to dial his number? *I wish we could start over.* His voice echoed and re-echoed in her ears.

She bit her lips. She had told him plainly that she didn't want him in her life right now. He was a man with a sense of almost Southern, old-fashioned courtesy. He'd accepted it. No, he wouldn't call her. The rules she'd learned about how a woman should be with a man stopped her from picking up the phone, from going to him.

How much of it was merely her stubborn pride? Did she nurture a fantasy of him crawling to her on his knees, begging and proffering diamonds because he couldn't live without her one minute more? No, that wasn't his style either. Or how much of her reluctance was simple embarrassment? She remembered the look in his eyes as he saw her at her worst. But he had come back and said he wanted her with him.

Was security and commitment more to her liking than compatibility, companionship and, yes, love? Were her fears more important? A few short days ago her pride thought they were. Now, she knew differently. She reached for her purse. She was going to him come what may.

* * *

Jason's car was gone. Tiffany pulled out her cellular phone and called his office. His receptionist told her he had just seen his last patient. He'd be coming home soon. Jason was a man of habit. She sat on his front porch in the porch glider she loved and curled her legs underneath her. She turned her face toward the sun and waited.

Almost an hour later he pulled up to the garage. He hit his brakes abruptly when he saw her car in the drive. A second later, he was striding toward her. He was such a beautiful man. The setting sun glowed behind him like a halo, and he almost looked like a god come to earth. Strength and gentleness combined with a potent brand of masculinity made Tiffany shiver at the memory of him.

She unfolded herself and stood. He stopped about a yard from her. *What if he sent her away? If he said no?*

She swallowed her fear and lifted her chin. "Jason. You know what you said about a chance to start all over. Well, that's what I'd like to do too."

An unbearable moment passed and she couldn't help a slight shiver. She'd bared her heart to him. How could she endure rejection?

He touched her cheek. "Let's go have a cup of coffee, dinner if you're hungry. We can talk."

She nodded, relief flooding her like a river and making her knees weak.

"I'll drive," he said.

They went to a quiet Italian restaurant. They ate pasta and talked of inconsequentials. Then Jason asked, "What made you change your mind?"

Tiffany looked away and then met his eyes. "I couldn't see throwing away a chance at happiness because of fear."

His eyes lit from within. "That's what wedged us apart—our fears, our history. We never talked about things. You never told me how you felt when your grandson died."

Tiffany laid her fork on her plate. "I felt like dying," she said. "I grieved my grandson, but it was deeper than that. It was a great source of my esteem that I was able to get my children past the legacy of dysfunction they were raised with. When I found out the extent of my failure with Dante . . . it was as if I had become nothing."

"You felt like you failed because of Dante's actions?"

"I accused him of being like his father. He said he was like me. A sorry drunk like I was. It was true, Jason. My daughter Jenny was a drunk and I found out my son turned out the same way. It was a poison in my blood that I passed on."

Tiffany felt tears welling in her eyes and looked away.

Jason took her hand. "I see the strength within you. The love, the care. From the bits and pieces I've heard, I gather that your husband was an abuser of the worst sort. The psychic wounds can take years to heal. You've all come an incredible way."

"I've gotten past that dark place where I was," she said. "I did get the help I needed. I realized that it's been a sign of weakness, not strength, that I've been reluctant to work on my issues. Jenny was right all along."

The waiter came and took their plates. "Coffee?" he asked.

"Yes, thanks," Jason said, and Tiffany nodded.

In a moment he brought steaming cups of coffee to them and Tiffany tipped the pitcher of cream and brought the warm liquid to her lips. Silence with Jason felt right sometimes. It never sat awkwardly between them, but lay like a cat stretched out in supreme comfort and confidence.

They'd almost finished their coffee before Jason spoke again. "I've been stuck in the past too. Diana's ghost haunted me because of guilt and fear of the new. I've laid her to rest. I've raised my children and it's time to move on. I just took an offer on the house."

"You're selling the house?" she breathed.

"It's time. I'm not saying it's not hard, but I need to move on."

The waiter brought them a check and Jason laid down a credit card. "I'll take you back to your car," he said.

They stood beside her car and Tiffany felt a physical need for this man so strong that she almost swayed toward him.

"What are you doing this weekend?" he asked.

The weekend was four days away. Far too long to go without seeing him. "I don't have plans."

"What do you think about amusement parks?"

"I don't think about them much."

Jason grinned. "They're having several good jazz bands at Six Flags Saturday night. Would you like to come with me?"

"That sounds wonderful."

"Good." He dropped a kiss on her forehead. "Drive home safely. I'm happy you came by." Then he walked away.

She stared after him for a moment before she clicked the remote to open her car door. She knew what he was doing: the courtship thing, getting to know one another without the overwhelming physical passion they had between them. Problem was she didn't know if she could take it. Right now she wanted that man's touch so bad it hurt. Four days until she saw him again seemed like an eternity.

Chapter 25

"Table for one?" the hostess asked Tiffany.

"I'm meeting someone. She's over there." Jenny sat in a booth, waving at her.

"Sorry I'm late," Tiffany said. "Something came up at the office at the last minute."

"That's all right. I haven't been here long," Jenny said.

The waiter appeared with menus. "I'm ready to order," Tiffany said. "I'd like a chef's salad and an iced tea."

"I'll have the same."

The waiter scratched on his pad and disappeared.

"So what did you have to tell me?" Tiffany asked.

Jenny took a sip of her water before answering. "It's about Dante."

Tiffany's gaze darted away. The waiter appeared with their iced tea, and she busied herself for a moment with the artificial sweetener while she steeled herself for the news. "What about Dante?"

"It was his first offense. He got a good lawyer and the

prosecution couldn't prove that his blood alcohol level contributed to the accident."

"So he's scot-free," Tiffany replied, her voice slightly bitter.

"Why are you so angry with him, Mom?"

"He lied to me. He made me believe he was something he wasn't."

"I disagree. Dante lied to himself. He was a man in denial until this happened."

"He walked away after his baby was killed. That's unforgivable. Cowardly."

"It was cowardly, but I think he was under extreme mental duress when he realized what he'd done. Like I said, Dante practiced denial, and reality had just given him a terrible blow."

The waiter brought their salads. "Dante has always tried to please, to seek approval," Jenny continued. "Remember how he was with Dad? And remember what happened when he finally confronted him?"

Tiffany closed her eyes. "Your father shot him."

"Now, that's what I call rejection," Jenny quipped.

"How can you joke about that?"

"I'm not joking. I'm trying to get you to see you're doing in essence the same thing Dad did, albeit in a less violent way. You're rejecting Dante."

"Do you realize what he said to me?"

"He told me."

"Do you agree with him? Did I fail you too?" Tiffany asked in a low voice.

Jenny touched her hand. "No, Mom, you never failed me. The times I've gotten into trouble, I failed myself. As did Dante. But there is something . . ."

"What's that?"

"You've stuffed the past under the rug, out of sight. It's major stuff we've never addressed as a family, a huge bump under the carpet. I think we're all still tripping over it. That's why we sometimes fall."

Tiffany toyed with her salad. Jenny was right. They never talked about what went on in the family when Sidney was alive. Tiffany had believed the painful past was better left behind as they all went forward with their lives. But it was still affecting them. What happened to Dante, and even her fear and self-doubt over the relationship with Jason—all specters from the past, unburied.

The events of the past three years, whatever they all were, had made profound changes in Jenny. Her daughter was a woman, tempered by fire. Three years ago, she'd been an often foolish, much more impulsive and self-centered girl. Now Jenny was strong enough to face her past. Was she? And what about Dante?

"What is Dante going to do now?" Tiffany asked.

"He quit his job. He lost his wife. Mom, I think he should come here and be with us. We need to heal as a family."

Tiffany nodded.

"But he won't because of you. He thinks you won't have anything more ever to do with him. You need to talk to him."

Tiffany said nothing.

"I know it's hard to forgive him, but he's your son. And he needs you."

"Dante is my son. I love him and always will. We do need to heal as a family. I'll go talk to him and try to bring him back with me."

Tiffany took the next day off work. Things had calmed down at work and she felt comfortable leaving her office in the ever-capable and eager hands of Janelle. The plane ticket she bought at the airline counter cost a fortune, but Dante was worth every penny. She hoped . . . She hoped a lot of things. That he would listen to her, that they could forgive each other, that he would come back with her so they could do the work needed to finally bury the past forever.

Tiffany clasped her hands together as she rode in the taxi from the airport toward Dante's place. Jenny had said Dante was staying in a little studio apartment and that he sounded very sad. Jenny reported that he'd mentioned he had no plans for the day. Tiffany prayed that he'd be home. They'd pulled up to a drab square building.

She paid the driver, but asked him to wait until she got in. She ran her finger down the row of names beside the buzzer until she came to her son's. She hesitated a moment and pressed the button.

"Yes?" His voice was tinny and small through the intercom.

"It's Mom."

Silence. Then the buzz of the door. She pulled it open and walked back into her son's life.

He stood at the door. "Why are you here?"

"I needed to talk to you."

He stepped aside and she walked into his apartment. Bare and clean, devoid of the slightest bit of warmth. She sat on the edge of the cheap sofa.

Dante pulled out a chair from the dinette and sat down. He folded his arms across his chest and waited.

"First I want to apologize for my anger. I don't expect you to understand it, but I want you to know that it's past. You're my son and I love you unconditionally. Always have and always will."

Dante looked down at his feet, visibly shaken.

"I appreciate you telling me that. I'm sorry I said what I did to you."

"It was true. Realization of my own failure is what made me react the way I did. It has much more to do with me than you. As did your father's actions."

Dante raised his head and stared at her. "You rarely mention Sidney's actions to me. I thought the topic was not a subject for discussion between us. The past died with Sidney, you'd say."

"I was wrong," Tiffany said, her voice low. "The past doesn't die, but it becomes a part of us. If we ignore it we can't control its expression. That's what happened to you."

Dante covered his face with his hands for a moment as if he was trying to shut out the memory. "I told myself I could lick my drinking myself if I could just keep it quiet enough."

He sighed. "The price has been too high. My son, my family, my life, all gone."

"Your son is gone, true. Celeste, too. But you are alive and breathing. You can make amends and make a difference in someone else's life."

"How can I do that, Mom? Look at me."

"Come back to St. Louis with me and let's face this together. Let's start over and do it right."

Jason woke and reached for Tiffany like he did every morning since she'd gone. All he grabbed was a leaden feeling of emptiness. He stared at the ceiling. It was finally Saturday morning. He'd stayed up late with his son watching a video movie last night. He felt it was much later than his usual time for rising. He moved his head and looked at the clock to verify that it was so. Eight in the morning.

He rolled out of bed and headed for the bathroom. Maybe he'd fallen into the twilight zone because the four days since he last saw Tiffany had taken four years to pass. It took every bit of his considerable self-discipline not to call her, not to take her in his arms every time he was close to her, and, God help him, not to take her to bed.

He would be at her front door to pick her up in exactly

three hours. He couldn't wait. He was putting toothpaste on his brush when the phone rang.

"Jason? This is Tiffany."

His pulse increased. Finally she called him. "Hi, Tiff," he managed to say with just the right amount of casualness.

"I'm sorry, but I'm not going to be able to make it this afternoon."

"What?" he said. His voice was too sharp. He swallowed and said more softly. "Why is that?"

"Dante has come here from Charlotte. We just got back yesterday and I don't feel it's right to leave him."

"So he didn't have a penalty?"

"His lawyer found proof of a possible error by the other driver, and Dante's blood alcohol level didn't necessarily contribute to the accident."

"So he got off."

"He was lucky. He got off with a slap on the wrist."

"Why did he come to St. Louis?"

"I went and got him. I need to make it up to him, Jason. He's my son, and my children are the most important things in the world to me."

Jason was silent, trying to understand, but deeply disappointed at not being able to see her. "You both have to eat, don't you? What about dinner?"

"I wanted to cook for him."

"Oh."

"I tell you what. Why don't you come by and have dinner with us?"

His spirits brightened considerably. "That sounds good."

"Around seven?"

"I'll be there. Do you need anything?"

"Just you," Tiffany said.

Jason's hands tightened on the phone. "You mean that?"

"I do. I'll see you tonight."

She hung up and he set the phone down on the cradle.

Why had she cancelled their date? Because she needed to baby-sit her twenty-seven-year-old son? It didn't make sense. Tiffany had confided in him how Dante's actions had rocked her sense of esteem, which was deeply rooted into being what she viewed as a good mother. He hoped she didn't go overboard with Dante, but he he feared she would. He and Tiffany needed time together. The future for them looked bleak unless they could communicate and trust one another fully. There was something about Tiffany he couldn't grasp. A slippery something that squirmed out of his grip every time he closed in on it. It was better now, but they still hadn't dealt with the demons that tore her from him when she faced her inner anguish. She should have been able to turn to him instead of to a bottle. He should have been able to offer her what she needed.

He didn't know if they could fix what was wrong between them: the lack of trust, the fear, and his reluctance to commit. But he wanted to try. He wanted it more than anything. But he felt a sense of foreboding that it wouldn't be enough.

Chapter 26

Tiffany had just put the cornmeal-coated catfish into the hot oil when there was a knock at her door. She frowned and wiped her hands on her jeans. When she pulled open the door, the small figure of the elderly woman who lived downstairs and owned the house, Grace Atchinson, stood there. "Come on in. Hold on a moment while I take care of this fish I was frying for dinner."

She turned off the fire and returned to the living room. "I like what you did to the apartment," Grace said.

"Thank you."

"I need to give you some news. I'm putting this place on the market. Your lease is still in effect of course and if you want to renew there's a possibility the buyers won't have a problem with it."

Tiffany's heart rose. "I'd love to buy this house. It's wonderful. What's your asking price?"

"Four and a half."

Tiffany's mouth dropped open. "Forty-five thousand

dollars?" If that were the case, she'd write out a check this instant.

Grace laughed. "This is Central West End, honey. Prime St. Louis real estate. Four hundred and fifty thousand."

Tiffany felt silly. She knew that. Her misunderstanding of what the woman said was just wishful thinking. She knew there was no way she could afford this house.

"That's an excellent asking price, by the way. I expect it'll go quickly. I need it to move fast."

"Why so soon?"

"My daughter took me to this retirement place. I said I'd never live in one of those places, but you should see this one. They have a chef and a spa with a massage room and even a bar. The old geezers don't look too bad either. It costs a bundle, but with what I'll get for this place, I can swing it. It'll be like living in Club Med."

"Well, I'm happy for you."

"I have to go and get things in order. So much to do. I just wanted to let you know. You take care of yourself now."

Tiffany looked after her as she bounded down the stairs with surprising agility for such an old lady. The place was going to be sold barely after she'd moved in. This house was her dream house. She loved everything about it. But it was out of reach. She shook her head as she went into the kitchen to finish cooking dinner for her son and Jason.

Dante was out with Jenny. She was getting him involved in some addiction treatment type things already. They'd agreed that next week she'd arrange family therapy. Intense family therapy. Because of the atmosphere of abuse that Sidney fostered and she had been too impaired to change, the term "dysfunctional family" was an understatement. They'd likely all be in therapy for years. So be it. She was determined to make amends and help her family become whole, at whatever cost.

* * *

Jason walked up the stairs to Tiffany's apartment promptly at seven. Great house, great location, he thought. Her son Dante answered the door. He looked different from the young man Jason had met weeks ago. The dark circles around this man's eyes and the weary expression on his face indicated that he was paying his dues.

"Hello, Jason. Come on in. Mom's in the kitchen."

"Good to see you again." Jason knew better than to ask him how things were going.

"Thanks. Good to see you too. Can I get you something to drink?"

"I'd appreciate that. I'm thirsty. Iced tea or water, please."

Dante disappeared into the kitchen as Tiffany emerged. She looked wonderful. Her boyish cut only accentuated the delicate femininity of her features, the fine shape of her head and the grace of her body. He wanted to fold her in his arms. There were times when she was a little prickly, a touch edgy, that contrasted with the overall gentle kindness and wisdom of her character. She was a natural nurturer. No wonder she'd gathered his motherless daughter Taylor under her wing.

He'd finally accepted everything, all of her. The past, the anger, the fear. It didn't matter. He was willing to go through any fire with her. What they needed was time to talk and to trust.

She approached with a smile that he hoped was telling him that she missed him as much as he missed her.

"It's good to see you again." She uttered the same words he had to Dante, but the deeper meaning beneath the words was unmistakable.

"Me too."

"I thought we'd eat in the kitchen. It's a huge kitchen. I love it."

"Sounds good," he murmured.

They gazed at each other. He needed to take her in his arms right this instant. He needed it more than breathing. She swayed to him, in tune with his thought. He moved toward her.

"Here's your iced tea," Dante said, handing him the glass.

"Er, thanks."

"Dinner's on the table. Let's eat before it gets cold."

Tiffany had prepared a simple meal of golden fried crunchy catfish, coleslaw and creamy au gratin potatoes. She topped it off with a huge slice of cherry pie à la mode.

Jason kept the conversation light, well away from the dark topics so near to the surface of their minds. He was curious about what Dante planned to do in St. Louis.

He observed Tiffany gazing at Dante, touching him at intervals as if to make sure he was really alive and well and with her. He knew how important her children were to her and how deeply her perceived failure with her son hurt her. But Dante was a grown man. A mother can't fix a man past a certain point. Beyond that was up to him.

"The owner is putting this house on the market," Tiffany said, her voice breaking into Jason's thoughts.

"So soon after you moved in?"

"She found a retirement community she wants to move into. I'd love to buy it, but it's way out of my price range."

"How much?"

"Four hundred and fifty thousand."

"It's a nice house," Jason said.

"I love it."

"I'm in the market for a house. Would you be offended if I looked into it?"

Tiffany laid down her fork. "You couldn't."

"Actually, I could, but I wouldn't if you had a problem with it."

Tiffany whooped and startled Jason so much he almost

knocked over his tea. "That would be fantastic! I wouldn't have to move. You're talking about an investment, right?"

"Well, yes."

Then the grin faded from her face. "You'd live here?"

"I might. But I wouldn't have to."

She picked her fork back up, subdued, considering. "You can go down and see Grace after dinner if you like."

"Sure. I'll see you afterward?" Jason asked.

Tiffany shifted in her seat. "I promised Dante I'd go to a meeting with him tonight."

Dante looked at Jason and smiled.

Two weeks later on a beautiful Saturday afternoon, Jason sat in his chair before the television. A game was on, but he paid it no mind. He was seriously worried. The past couple of weeks he'd barely gotten to spend a second alone with Tiffany. Trying to see her had also been a hassle. She had meetings almost every evening of the week, and Dante occupied the rest of her time. He'd tried to be patient, he'd tried to understand, but he'd about had enough.

He'd planned this old-fashioned courtship of getting to know each other again. He wanted to do it right this time instead of jumping into a sizzling sexual relationship that overshadowed everything else, as they had done before. He wanted to have fun together. Deepen their intimacy. It wasn't working. Her son was the main problem. The few times that Jason was with her, Dante was always there with them, enveloped in a morose cloud of depression.

Tiffany had her hands too full trying to deal with Dante and face her own and her family's issues in the therapy they'd initiated. Dante refused to go into residential treatment. Tiffany had confided to Jason it was as if Dante was going through the motions, just there for the ride. She was afraid to leave him alone, she'd said. What kept Jason going was the longing in her eyes when she looked at him across the room.

He'd been patient, but this had gone on too long. Dante was a man, around the age of his own sons. He'd never let behavior like this from one of them go on without his intervention, no matter what trauma they'd been through. Jason clicked the television off. It was time he and Dante had a talk.

He called Tiffany's apartment and Dante answered the phone. "Hi, Jason. Mom stepped out to go to the store."

"I didn't call for your mom, I called for you. I want to ask you out for some coffee. I'd like to talk to you."

"I don't drink coffee."

"Tea then." A note of firmness entered Jason's voice, the note he used to let his sons know they were teetering near the edge.

"All right, I guess. Mom will be worried to find me gone."

"Leave her a note. I'll be there in ten minutes."

Dante sat across from Jason at the trendy coffeehouse nursing a cup of herb tea. Jason noted that he looked visibly nervous. Dante was a pleasant-looking young man of average height but muscular build. His features were open and intelligent despite the cloud of lethargy and depression that hung over him.

Jason wasn't sure what he was going to say, but he approached it the same way he approached a difficult surgery. He relied on his knowledge and experience, did the best he possibly could, and turned the outcome over to God. "So what are your long-range plans here in St. Louis?" he asked.

"I don't really know yet. Right now I'm just trying to get back on my feet."

"Are you?"

"Excuse me?" Dante asked, clearly puzzled.

"Are you getting back on your feet? You seem to be a man with considerable potential."

"I guess so." Dante took a sip of his tea and frowned at either the heat or the taste of it. "So what did you want to talk to me about?"

"I wanted to get more of a feel for you and what you're going through. You know I have an ulterior motive."

"My mother."

"Yes. She's worried about you."

"She worries too much."

"Why do you let her? You're a man."

"Yes, I'm a man. That's the whole point of this little talk, isn't it? 'Dante, get your act together and leave your mother and me alone.' You don't care about me."

Jason sipped his coffee and savored the flavor. It was perfect. It should be for the cost. "First of all," he said, "I don't allow my sons to use profanity when they speak to me and I'm not going to allow you to do so either." Jason gazed at Dante until he dropped his eyes.

"There's a grain of truth in what you say," he continued. "But the part about me not caring is wrong. You are the son of a woman I care for a great deal. She told me your father was terribly abusive to you and treated you with disrespect your entire life when he wasn't ignoring you. I felt sorry for you. That's a part of the reason that I'm here talking to you."

"I never asked for your pity," Dante snarled.

"At the rate you're going, you've got it whether you asked for it or not," Jason said in a pleasant voice. He caught the eye of the waitress, who hurried over. "Can I have one of your whole wheat nut doughnuts? Do you want one, Dante? They're good."

"No."

He turned his attention back to Dante when the waitress left. "Like I said, the reason I wanted to talk to you was to get a feel for who you are. My motive is to see if there is anything I can do to help you and if you'd accept my help, primarily to take some of the strain off your mother. I made no assumptions; I wanted to explore the issue. I'm the sort of man who when faced with a problem I try to do something about it." The waitress brought him his doughnut and he dunked it in his coffee. "Are you?" he asked.

Dante's silence was sullen, hostile.

Jason sighed and took a bite of his doughnut. "I guess not," he said.

"Your mother feels responsible for your well-being. She's taken it upon herself, not realizing that you are the only person who can make a difference in your life. You're past the point where she can fix you. She needs to understand this."

Dante shrugged and Jason's pity turned into compassion. This was a young man in deep pain. He hoped the best for him, but if he decided to go down, he wasn't dragging Tiffany down with him, not if Jason had anything to do with it.

"Check, please," Jason said to the waitress.

Chapter 27

Jason signed the papers at the house closing with a flourish. He was the new owner of Grace Atchinson's former home. He hadn't told Tiffany how far his negotiations with the house had gone. He wanted to surprise her. He knew how much she loved the house and her apartment.

The past week, he'd been able to spend more time with her. Dante had understandably made himself scarce when Jason was around. Jason sensed that Tiffany needed no heavy conversation, much less confrontations about Dante. She needed a listening ear, a shoulder to lean on. She needed small pleasures and to get away from the problem Dante was coming to be. He provided these things gladly.

His beeper went off and he saw Tiffany's home phone number. Tiffany hardly ever beeped him. He reached for his cellular phone.

"Jason, can you come by now? I need you." Her voice was raw and hoarse.

"I'll be right there."

A few minutes later, she pulled open the door at the

moment his finger touched the doorbell. Tiffany's eyes were red-rimmed, her face anguished. She walked into his arms and he enfolded them around her. He felt her trembling like a tiny bird. He ran a hand over her hair. "What's wrong, baby?" he asked.

"It's Dante. He's been drinking. I found a flask in his room."

"Where is he now?"

"I don't know. Oh God, Jason, I tried so hard with him. I'm worthless as a mother."

He grasped her arms. "Stop it. It's not true. You've been a wonderful mother. You've done all you could and more. You can't fix Dante or Jenny or anybody once they're grown. They have to fix themselves. All you can do is love them. That's all you have to do. At a certain point you turn your children over. Dante's well past that point. He is responsible for his actions. Not you. Do you understand me? Dante is a man. Let him be one, stand or fall."

"Why are you talking about me?" Dante said from the open door.

Jason swung around. Tiffany turned and picked up a pint of liquor from the table. She handed it to him. "That's why," she said.

Jason noted with relief that already she seemed calmer.

Conflicting emotions ran over Dante's face. Finally he said to his mother, "I'm sorry."

"I am too. Dante, you'll have to move out if you're drinking. I can't have it under my roof."

"Yes." He looked at his mother. "I guess it's the end of the road for me, huh? You probably hate me now."

She moved toward him and embraced him. He stood stiff for a moment, then he seemed to crumple into her. He buried his face on her shoulder. "I'm so sorry, Mom."

When he lifted his head, she touched his cheek. "I love you no matter what, Dante. Just because I asked you to move out doesn't mean I love you a bit less than I did before. You are my son. That will never change and neither will the way I feel about you."

Dante's head dropped. He stared at his feet. "I heard you telling my mother to let me be a man," he said without raising his head.

"Yes, I did."

He raised his head and looked at Jason. "I'm going to ask you to take me to the alcohol treatment center the therapist and Jenny recommended. I'm tired of hurting everybody I love."

Jason reached in his pocket for his keys and followed Dante out the door.

Tiffany touched her lips as she watched the two men she loved most in the world walk out the door together. She sank on the sofa and curled her legs under her. She had wondered what she would do if Dante started drinking again despite everything she'd been trying to do for him. She hadn't known if she could endure it.

When it happened, it was as if she descended into an abyss again. But this time she reached out to Jason. She'd finally taken her deepest cares and anxieties to Jason, and he'd soothed her like nobody ever had before. And even though nothing had changed, everything was all right. She'd known what she had to do. She closed her eyes in a silent prayer of thanks for having been gifted with such a man. The fear she felt, the doubt, the insecurity . . . it was gone, replaced by love. She was ready to lay to rest those ghosts of the past.

A little while later, when he returned, she walked into his arms again. "I think he's going to be all right," Jason murmured.

"I wish so."

He gazed at her for a moment before his head bent and his lips covered hers. They met each other as if they'd been denied air. Gasping with need. Ravenous. He raised his head, his eyes dark with passion. "I didn't want to do this."

He couldn't be serious, she thought.

"I wanted to wait. I wanted everything to be perfect and planned. I wanted all the loose threads tied and everything settled between us. I need to make love to you right now more than I need anything in the world, but it wasn't supposed to be like this."

She caressed the expanse of his chest. "I need you. As far as I'm concerned, everything is settled. There's been a change in me."

"What's that?"

"Realization. Gratitude. You've seen me at my very worst and you came back to me. You've always been there for me like a rock. Now, I can trust, and I trust you more than I've trusted any human being before. You are everything to me, Jason Cates."

He kissed her then, wild, sweet and tender. Their clothes fell to the floor, skin craving skin. Passion too long denied ignited and soon blazed out of control. When he entered her, Tiffany gasped with the wonder of it. His body urged hers to heights she'd never before reached and they cried out their completion to one another.

Later, he propped himself on his elbow over her and traced the outline of her lips. "Tiffany, I love you and I need you. I can't do without you anymore."

He kissed her lips lightly, softly, like a butterfly. "I accept and love you just the way you are now. I love you every bit as much as I ever loved Diana, and now since I have more age and hopefully more wisdom, I'm able to love you more."

A smile of sheer happiness curved her lips. "I love you too. You know that. The only fear I have left is the fear of losing you."

"There is no life without the possibility of loss. I can

promise to be by your side for the rest of my life, supporting, caring for you and loving you whatever happens. I
can't control life's river. Nobody can. I could die tomorrow.
So could you or anyone. But love negates fear. Marry me
and let's gamble on love for the rest of our lives."

Marry me. She reached out to him. The waters of the
past carried her. They flowed forward and she stepped
into the tumultuous river of Jason's love and life and
rushed toward the promises of the unknown future together.

"Yes," she whispered.

Dear Readers,

I could think of few characters that deserved a second chance at love more than Tiffany, whose story begins in HEART'S DESIRE. In that book we meet Tiffany, Jenny and Dante for the first time and witness the past events referred to in NEVER TOO LATE FOR LOVE. The Eastman family's lives and loves will continue with Jenny's story in an upcoming book.

Jason's friend Marvin, his new wife Edna, and her daughter Carmel are featured in THE LOOK OF LOVE. Taylor and Stone's courtship is consummated in A MAGICAL MOMENT. I especially enjoyed bringing so many characters from my past books into this story and I hope you do too.

Contact me at *monica@monicajackson.com* and be sure and take a peek at my web page at *http://www.monicajackson.com* for my views and upcoming news.

Good reading and much love always,
Monica Jackson

Coming in July from Arabesque Books . . .

__ISLAND MAGIC by Bette Ford
1-58314-113-8   **$5.99US/$7.99CAN**

When Cassandra Mosely needs a break from her work—and from her relationship with Gordan Kramer—she vacations in Martinique and finds herself in a new romance. But Gordan is determined to win her back and with a little island magic, the two just may rediscover their love . . .

__IMAGES OF ECSTASY by Louré Bussey
1-58314-115-4   **$5.99US/$7.99CAN**

Shay Hilton is shocked when her ex-fiancé is murdered in her apartment, but when she comes face to face with her prosecutor, Braxton Steele, she is overcome with desire. When a storm traps the unlikely couple together, it's the beginning of a passion that will change both of their lives forever . . .

__FAMILY TIES by Jacquelin Thomas
1-58314-114-6   **$5.99US/$7.99CAN**

When Dr. McKenzie Ashford discovers that her new boss, Marc Chandler, may be responsible for her mother's death, she is determined to obtain justice. She never imagines that her quest might uncover long-hidden family secrets . . . or that her heart might be overcome with love for Marc.

__SNOWBOUND WITH LOVE by Alice Wootson
1-58314-148-0   **$5.99US/$7.99CAN**

After a car accident, Charlotte Thompson develops a case of amnesia and seeks comfort in the arms of her handsome rescuer, Tyler Fleming. But as they fall in love, Tyler realizes her true identity as the person he holds responsible for the tragedy that nearly destroyed his life. Will he be able to give his heart to this woman that he has hated for so long?

Call toll free **1-888-345-BOOK** to order by phone or use this coupon to order by mail. *ALL BOOKS AVAILABLE JULY 1, 2000.*

Name_____

Address _____

City_____ State _____ Zip _____

Please send me the books I have checked above.

I am enclosing $_____

Plus postage and handling* $_____

Sales tax (in NY, TN, and DC) $_____

Total amount enclosed $_____

*Add $2.50 for the first book and $.50 for each additional book.
Send check or money order (no cash or CODs) to: **Arabesque Books, Dept. C.O., 850 Third Avenue, 16th Floor, New York, NY 10022**
Prices and numbers subject to change without notice.
All orders subject to availability.

Visit our website at **www.arabesquebooks.com**